D0016569

TORCHWOOD

ALMOST PERFECT

The *Torchwood* series from BBC Books:

1. ANOTHER LIFE
   Peter Anghelides

2. BORDER PRINCES
   Dan Abnett

3. SLOW DECAY
   Andy Lane

4. SOMETHING IN THE WATER
   Trevor Baxendale

5. TRACE MEMORY
   David Llewellyn

6. THE TWILIGHT STREETS
   Gary Russell

7. PACK ANIMALS
   Peter Anghelides

8. SKYPOINT
   Phil Ford

9. ALMOST PERFECT
   James Goss

TORCHWOOD
ALMOST PERFECT

James Goss

2 4 6 8 10 9 7 5 3 1

Published in 2008 by BBC Books, an imprint of Ebury Publishing
A Random House Group company

Torchwood is a BBC Wales production for BBC Two
Executive Producers: Russell T Davies and Julie Gardner

Original series created by Russell T Davies and broadcast on BBC Television

The Random House Group Limited Reg. No. 954009.
Addresses for companies within the Random House Group can be found at www.randomhouse.co.uk.

A CIP catalogue record for this book is available from the British Library.

ISBN 978 1 846 07573 5

The Random House Group Limited supports The Forest Stewardship Council (FSC), the leading international forest certification organisation. All our titles that are printed on Greenpeace approved FSC certified paper carry the FSC logo. Our paper procurement policy can be found at www.rbooks.co.uk/environment

Commissioning Editor: Albert DePetrillo
Series Editor: Steve Tribe
Production Controller: Phil Spencer

Cover design by Lee Binding @ Tea Lady © BBC 2008
Typeset in Albertina and Century Gothic
Printed in Great Britain by Clays Ltd, St Ives plc

FIVE RARE TIMES THAT IANTO JONES SWEARS*

1. The woman is looking at her burning hands. And she's screaming. And Ianto sees what she sees.
2. It's like being inside a giant washing machine. The back of the ferry is wide open and water is pouring in. And the water's cold and filthy and the loading bay is turning, and Ianto is suddenly looking at a lorry. One of them is upside down. And then suddenly, it doesn't matter.
3. The man is sat at a table in the restaurant. It's got a lovely view of Cardiff Bay. The food is laid out before him. The champagne is fizzing in the glass. He sits there, immaculately dressed. He is a skeleton.
4. Ianto thought he wouldn't see anything more disturbing at the club. But then – who paints their walls the colour of blood? And then he leans against it and realises the wall is breathing.
5. It's Monday morning. The alarm goes off. Ianto wanders into the bathroom, switches on the light and…

* *in no particular order*

RHYS IS SUNDAY SHOPPING WITH THE MISSUS

Rhys was delighted. 'Look, Gwen, I've found you an alien!'

Gwen looked up from a crap jewellery stand. Towering over them was a street performer, covered in metal plate and body armour. Silver tendrils spilled out of the top of his head. 'Yes, love,' she said. 'If only it was that easy.'

A crowd was watching the alien, who must have been almost three metres tall. There was a grim nobility about the performance – a stern refusal to move or even acknowledge the shoppers. The alien had a pitch on Queen Street, just away from a man singing into a traffic cone, a cluster of mobile phone shops and some students handing out free samples of a new cereal bar.

A man rolled up next to the alien and opened up his stall of ties, watches and sunglasses. The crowd's attention wandered slightly. Ever professional, the alien shifted its weight subtly, a mass of heaving tendrils drifting across from behind its head. A small child shrieked, which aroused some 'oohs'.

Rhys was entranced. Gwen giggled. 'What are you like?'

Rhys shrugged. 'Well, yeah – but he's very good isn't he? Way better than the Chaplin that used to be here. I know he's made those flappy things out of an old mop, but he's done it well, hasn't he?'

'Suppose,' Gwen's eye was caught by one of the suited children working at a mobile shop. He was edging closer with leaflets and a smile. She shuddered and started to steer Rhys away by the elbow.

'Funny, isn't it?' said Rhys, not quite moving with her. This was the start of a little routine with him, as ritual as the way he licked his knife after buttering toast. 'If he were a real alien, we'd all run screaming. But here he is, and we're all... you know... interested... but a bit bored. Not scared.'

'Yeah yeah – it's an integration scheme run by the Tourist Board. Now let's go stretch a pound.'

Rhys finally moved away. And as they went, Gwen glanced back at the alien.

It winked.

1. STATUS UPDATES

EMMA WEBSTER IS...

Emma Webster is still looking for love.
Emma Webster is watching Desperate Housewives (again!!!!)
Emma Webster is looking forward to Friday.
Emma Webster is going out again!!!
Emma Webster is recovering.
Emma Webster is hating Monday.
Emma Webster is fancying the new boy.
Emma Webster is flirting.
Emma Webster is getting somewhere.
Emma Webster is going for a drink with the new boy!
Emma Webster isn't the type to kiss and tell.
Emma Webster is going for a long walk in the sunshine.
Emma Webster is all excited.
Emma Webster is seeing him again.
Emma Webster is unable to remember what the film was about.
Emma Webster is going out for a drink with the girls.
Emma Webster is buying a little black dress.
Emma Webster isn't sure what happened there.
Emma Webster is forgetting about the diet.
Emma Webster is avoiding him.

Emma Webster is grateful for the calls.
Emma Webster is not going to text him.
Emma Webster is thinking of getting a cat.
Emma Webster is staying in.
Emma Webster is home to the folks.
Emma Webster is bored out of her mind.
Emma Webster is sick of 'why can't you settle down like your sister?'
Emma Webster isn't afraid of the big three-oh.
Emma Webster is making a change.

EMMA WEBSTER HAS A PLAN FOR A BRAND NEW ME

Emma was out jogging. Like most new plans in Emma's life it had required shopping. Shopping for lovely trainers, a nice sports bra and the dinkiest music player on the market. In pink, of course. She'd set off late, but managed to make it from Grangetown down through the Bay and off towards Penarth. It was dark, she was out of breath, her feet hurt, she kept having little breaks, and she was sweating like an old tea bag. But she had Girls Aloud in her ears and she was convinced the fat was melting off her thighs.

And that was when Emma saw the body on the beach. The street lights were bad, but it was unmistakeable. Lying on the rocks was the most beautiful woman she'd ever seen. Emma scrambled over, her music still playing as she stood over the body. Emma had never been good with dead animals. One of her earliest memories was of the cat leaping onto her bed with a dead vole. Her reaction was similar now – she just stood there, whimpering a little. She breathed really deeply, knelt down and, screwing her eyes shut, reached out to touch the corpse. Oh god, oh god, oh my god… It felt normal. A bit cold and a lot wet, but normal. Emma opened one eye. There was a chance the body wasn't dead.

Emma stood up and screamed for help, but it was Sunday

night and no one was around. She didn't have her mobile – it was just her, a body, and the tinny sound of 'Something Kinda Oooh' leaking from her headphones.

Emma felt for a pulse – there was one. Gentle, quiet, and faint. She ran her fingers up and down the woman's neck, distracted for just a second by how... perfect it was. She struggled to remember how to do CPR. It was something to do with pressing down on the chest several times and then giving the kiss of life. But how many times to do each thing? She remembered practising at work on a dummy – a weird old thing that whiffed of TCP and made a noise like a creaking bed when you pressed down on it. This was different. No noise. Just a strange wet feeling as she pushed the chest. When she tilted back the head and tried to breathe into it, a small trickle of water came out. Kissing her felt funny – and must have seemed bloody weird to anyone watching. But Emma kept on – pushing on the chest and breathing into those full, dead lips.

It was actually quite dull, despite her rising feeling of oh god-oh god panic. She was convinced she'd done it for hours, but when she checked her watch it turned out to be a couple of minutes. And no sign of life. On TV, some hunky doctor would be brushing her out of the way, yelling 'Clear!' and applying the shock pads. But this was just Emma. Alone.

With nothing but the beach and the woman, Emma started to notice things. Like the fact that the woman was wearing man's clothes. Quite a good suit, soaked through, though. She carried on pushing down on the – really firm – chest. It all felt weird. Those cold, cold lips, kissing a corpse. How had the woman even got here? All that beauty and here she was, poor thing, dead on a beach. She could only be in her mid twenties.

Eventually, she spread the woman out and sat back on her heels, exhausted. She'd tried to save a life and she'd failed. The wind was getting up, and the waves were slapping at the rocks around them. Everything smelt of oil and rotting seaweed.

Emma felt colder than she'd ever felt before.

It was then that she noticed the object clutched in the woman's hand. About the size of an iPod, but like a flat snowglobe, glowing slightly. Curious, Emma took it from the woman's grasp and held it up to the light – it was filled with a liquid that was a complicated blue that formed dancing shapes. As she looked into the globe she realised the shapes were straight lines and right angles and knotted cubes and so many shapes and colours and more shapes and—

Hey there, baby doll.

'What?' Emma gasped. She spun round. There was no one else on the beach with her. No one, anywhere. Even her music was silent. She was utterly alone. But still she was breathing quickly with shock.

Oi! I am speaking to you, darlin'.

The voice was female, strong, northern and very definitely in her head.

I'm the machine.

This time there was a sigh. It was the long-suffering sigh that gave it away.

'Cheryl?' Emma gulped. What was Cheryl from Girls Aloud doing in her head?

Yeah. Right. Finally! I'm merely a representation of the machine's mental interface, babe. You just listen up and Cheryl will give you an exclusive.

'This machine?' Emma shook it. Her head filled with a shriek.

Hold on there, sister! That will not happen again! Understand? You get me, you stupid little bitch?

'Oi!' Emma was outraged. 'Why are you in my head? What are you?'

The voice seemed calmer, more soothing.

Well now. This will take some explaining. Shall we go somewhere warm and snug so we can get to know each other better?

'What about the body I found y—?' Emma didn't even get to finish the sentence.

Oh, don't worry about that – that was just a civilian. It brought me ashore. It'll wake up in a bit, go home, get some kip, forget all this happened. Now come on – let's get back to your charming one-bedroom flat in Grangetown with an eighty-five per cent mortgage and talk about the future. Let's just say there's a lot in it for you, Emma darling.

'What?' Cheryl had an odd way of speaking, thought Emma.

Hey, sorry, babe. It's just my way. Forgive me, yeah? Cheryl is your favourite, isn't she? Would you prefer if I was Nicola?

Emma thought about it. 'No,' she said.

So, Emma found herself turning away from the woman's body and walking off the beach and back to her flat. Oddly, neither she nor the machine spoke to each other on the way – although the voice was humming along to the tune on her iPod. Thinking about it, Emma couldn't remember much about the walk. But suddenly there she was, sat on her sofa, staring at her coffee table which contained the machine and a mug of her favourite instant hot chocolate (Midnight Orange Murmur, since you ask).

Well now, this is cosy.

'Yeah,' said Emma, feeling a touch defensive.

But it could be better. Don't yer think? There was something about the voice – it was all caring and bright, but there was a real touch of steel behind it. But perhaps that was just Cheryl. *And that's what I'm here for. Let's just say I'm a real dream machine, sweetheart.*

'So, you're like a genie? And I get three wishes?'

A tinkle of laughter. *Oh, Emma, honey, you get waaaaay more than three wishes. I just have to look into your mind and I can give you what you want. I can make you what you've always dreamed of. Taller, thinner, better hair. Darling, there's no limit to what you can achieve with knockout tits and a nice smile.*

Emma reached out a trembling hand for her mug and took an uncertain sip of her chocolate. There was an excited fluttering in her stomach. 'Really? Does it hurt? How much does it cost?'

Ah, that's the best bit. There's no cost. I'm just chuffed to be able to help. And it's started already. Want to see what you can look like? Go on girl – take a butcher's in the mirror.

Emma stood up and crossed to the wicker-framed lounge mirror. And she dropped her mug in shock. She bolted off to the kitchen and returned with a damp cloth. She scrubbed away at the carpet, staring at herself in the mirror and repeating over and over 'oh my god oh my god oh my god oh my god' while the voice of Cheryl giggled delightedly in her head.

When she was eventually satisfied that there wouldn't be a stain, she stood up, nervously straightening out her jogging trousers and staring at herself. She turned sideways and then sneaked a look at her bum.

And, finally, Emma laughed. She was suddenly gorgeous. Her figure was firmer, taller, and her eyes bluer – and yet she was still herself. She felt warm and confident and brilliant, and her skin was radiant.

And that, Em, is just the start of what we can do. We're gonna have such a laugh. Things are going to be just perfect.

GWEN IS LATE FOR WORK

Gwen was late for reasons that bored even her. She briefly toyed with an apology to Jack that took in Rhys's eccentric approach to whites-only laundry, but figured 'life is too, too short'. So she slumped down at her desk, grabbed a bite of her Greggs pastry thing, logged in to the baffling swirl of her Torchwood desktop, and then noticed the New And Upsetting Thing.

'Er, hello!' she said, grinning broadly at the stunning woman tidying a workstation.

The woman looked up briefly, smiled weakly, and went back to watering the plants.

Bitch, thought Gwen. She'd clearly missed a memo. First Martha, now this. Replacing Owen with some ice queen with no personality, great hair and bloody amazing shoes. Gwen decided this was the worst Monday at Torchwood ever. Working with a supermodel. Great. Goodbye biscuits, booze and Primark. Hello gym, bottled water and clothes she couldn't afford. What was Jack thinking?

She sneaked a glance across the desk. Actually, she knew exactly what Jack was thinking. For a man who'd lived through the entire twentieth century, he sometimes seemed stuck in the Dark Ages. Gwen breathed in. Better make friends. You never know, she might be genuinely nice, or she might get horrid period pains or have a really bad stutter. Poor lamb. Thinking about it, hell, she worked for Torchwood – she was bound to have lost half her family and everyone she'd ever kissed.

'Hiya!' Gwen said again.

'What?' said the woman, looking up. She looked odd. Distracted, but also a bit... no, not shy... embarrassed. Why? She hadn't farted or something had she? Oh, please let it be that. Please.

'Is everything OK?' ventured Gwen, trying to keep the smile out of her voice.

'What do you think?' the woman snapped back, miserably. 'I look like this! It is definitely not OK.'

'Oh, I don't know,' said Gwen, trying to sound sympathetic. 'I think you look very nice,' she finished, sounding like her Aunt Phyliss outside Sunday chapel. Please tell me she's not about to start ranting about feeling fat. I am so going to hate her.

'Nice?' snorted the woman. 'Not you too. Honestly, you turn up with a short skirt, and suddenly everyone's trying to jump you. Typical Torchwood.'

Gwen blinked. 'Excuse me, I think you're mistaken. I'm, ah, definitely not trying to have...' What would they say in a real office? Er... 'Oh god. I'm not flirting with you. I am simply saying that I think that you're looking... quite nice. Yes.' Gwen finished the sentence and vowed never to start another one. There. It probably hadn't gone too badly – the poor thing was probably constantly being hit on. Easy mistake to make, etc, olive branch extended. Lovely.

'Oh, please, get over yourself, Gwen,' snapped the woman, miserably. 'You don't understand a thing.'

'Is that so?' Gwen felt herself puffing up. The woman started to smile, smile in a way that Gwen decided would go really well with a slap. As the red mist started to descend, Gwen heard the thundering of boots on the metal gantry behind her.

'Gwen!' yelled Jack. 'Gwen!'

Gwen turned. 'What?' she snapped.

'It's not what you think!' said Jack.

'No, it's not,' said the woman, looking a little scared. Good. Hang on. There was something familiar. A little sad, even.

Gwen looked back at the woman. 'Do I know you?'

The woman shrugged helplessly.

'Gwen, this is Ianto,' said Jack.

'Bloody Torchwood,' said Gwen.

EMMA IS HAVING HER LAST BAD DAY AT WORK

Emma took a drag on her cigarette and looked up at the office. The voice in her head was telling her marvellous things. And she believed them.

She couldn't quite get over the changes in her. It was like she'd been on one of those TV programmes, only without the agonising surgery and patronising humiliation. She was calling today Makeover Day, the day she made a real difference at work.

Interestingly, people had only gradually noticed the change in her, which disappointed her slightly.

It will take people who know you a day to adjust. And that's a good thing, trust me. They'll just come away thinking you're looking good. We don't want them getting suspicious. Life is not just a case of taking off your glasses and throwing back your hair and but Miss Jones you're beautiful. We'll have none of that crap, ta very much.

'Oh,' Emma had thought. 'Not even a little?'

Oh, buck up, sweetheart. True class never makes a grand entrance. Just be the natural centre of attention.

And yet, the morning had passed with barely a comment – good hair, nice dress, was that a new herbal tea she was drinking? But nothing to stop the world. The thing is, there was only one reaction she was waiting for – Vile Kate's.

But Vile Kate hadn't even noticed. 'Ooh, you shouldn't eat that, not now you've passed the big three-oh!' she'd said. Vile Kate was always saying things like that. Always pottering surreptitiously around the office with large cards with nasty drawings of teddies on them, her life an endless round of collecting together presents for leaving-dos and birthdays and weddings and births and Secret-sodding-Santa.

Kate was, as far as everyone else seemed to think, the jolliest, nicest person in the office. She had a lovely new boyfriend ('Maurice' pronounced 'Maw-reece'), an almost endless bundle of kiddies, and a natural ability to succeed at work without either intelligence or effort. And yet Emma hated and feared Vile Kate.

And this was because of her stunning talent at swatting her down without effort: 'Aw, sweets – you're all out of breath. Of course you'll be like that if you keep smoking.' Or: 'Oh dear. You're looking tired. Are you all right?'

Everyone liked Kate. No one really liked Emma. Not that that was a real problem – it was just work. It hadn't been a problem in Bristol. Emma had had loads of mates back in Bristol. She'd loved living there. Well, until she and Paul had split up. They'd been really amicable about it, and it had been easier moving to the Cardiff branch when the chance of a tiny promotion had come up. She still saw him loads, and they still hung out with the same bunch of friends a couple of times a month. It was all great. It was just taking her a while to find friends of her own in Cardiff. Which had meant a lot of quiet nights in, or nights out with the girls from work. Everyone at work (apart from Kate) was lovely. They were just a bit… you know, All Bar One.

Emma had been trying to learn a bit about rugby and to like the flavour of Brains followed rapidly by zambuca. She was already a master of staggering down Chippie Alley in search of a kebab and a taxi.

'I see you're doing that speed-dating, love,' continued Kate, looming over her desk. She had one of those voices, a constant tone of mildly resentful surprise. Emma imagined she'd use the same tone for 'Ooh, I hear you've joined the Nazi Party.'

Emma stared dead ahead at her computer and let the remark hang in the air. Don't respond. Don't join in. Don't… you know. Let her win.

'Exciting,' continued Kate with a little laugh at nothing. 'Well, I think it's nice if you've not managed to find a man in the usual manner.' Another little laugh.

Emma felt herself blushing and stared directly into her Outlook, willing a new email to turn up. She kept her smile effortlessly in place.

I'll show you, she thought.

Oh yes, said the surprising voice in her head. *We'll show her.*

IANTO IS MORE IMPORTANT THAN STATIC CLING

Gwen and Jack sat in the boardroom, trying not to look at Ianto as he came in with a tray of coffee.

'How?' she mouthed.

Jack shrugged.

Ianto leaned forward to pass over a cup and Gwen boggled. She mimed melons to Jack. He nodded.

Ianto looked between the two of them, stiffly.

'OK, team!' said Jack. 'It's a busy day. Lots to cover. Ianto's a woman, a ferry nearly sank and static electricity is up by twenty-three per cent.'

'What's top priority?' asked Gwen.

'Ianto,' boomed Jack. 'Unless you're wearing nylon.'

'OK,' said Gwen. 'How did he… she…? I mean…'

Ianto shrugged. 'I just woke up like this. No memory, slight hangover, pair of breasts. Honestly.'

Gwen nodded. 'Right. Nothing unusual then?'

'Well, not apart from the surprising lack of cock.'

'A situation we can all sympathise with,' sighed Jack. 'Ianto Jones is brilliant, you know. He wakes up. Different fingerprints, voice, DNA, so how am I going to recognise him? He kisses me. And I know at once! Isn't that the most romantic thing you've ever heard?' He grinned dopily.

Ianto looked embarrassed. 'It really is me Gwen. I really don't know how I can prove it to you, but—'

'Please don't kiss me!' Gwen protested, giggling and waving him away. 'Are you sure you're OK?'

'I'm fine. Confused, mildly frightened, but basically fine.' Ianto nodded. 'It's me, Gwen. If I'm a cunning alien infiltration plan, then I'm the worst ever.'

Jack smiled. 'We'll sort it out. We always do. Somehow. Don't you worry, Ianto Jones.'

'Thank you. To be honest,' admitted Ianto, 'bit freaked.'

'Yes, but, on the scale of things, it's hardly another nuclear blast in Aberdare. It's more for our HR department.'

Gwen looked troubled. 'But we don't have an HR department.'

'We've got you,' said Jack, and smirked.

Gwen didn't rise to it. Instead she patted Ianto on the arm. 'We can solve this. This is nothing – we got you back from being invisible.'

Ianto nodded, his hair cascading neatly down his shoulders. 'And now I'm the Highly Visible Woman.' There was a little of his old voice in his laugh.

Gwen glanced at Jack. 'We should start with his memory, shouldn't we?'

Jack nodded approvingly. 'There is something I had in mind, yes.'

Ianto looked alarmed. 'Oh. You're going to use something alien on me, aren't you?'

Jack nodded. 'Kind of. It's an anti-retcon pill. Supposed to reverse memory loss.'

'But…?'

Jack pulled the pill out of a pocket and picked some fluff off of it. 'It'll take a while to start working. If it works at all. Maybe three days. Sooner if there's a trigger. Plus, there's a tiny danger that you might remember Everything.'

'What's wrong about tha- oh.'

'Yup,' said Jack. 'It's not selective. You might suddenly have a head full of maths tests and Monday mornings.'

Ianto smiled bravely. 'Who's to say I don't already?' He took the pill, which tasted pleasantly fruity.

'Hmm,' said Jack. 'Hope that was the right pill.' He patted down his pockets. 'Ah well. Let me know if you start seeing clowns.'

'Right,' said Ianto quietly. 'Well, let's wait and see.' He looked around the room. 'What's next?'

'The ferry crash. Well, by all accounts, more of a ferry prang, really. Although that hasn't stopped David Brigstocke calling it "a major maritime disaster" on Radio Wales.'

'Tosser,' tutted Gwen and Ianto together.

Jack stood up. 'We should get going.'

Ianto remained seated. 'Can I stay behind? If that's all right? I'd like a chance to, you know, work on my memory. Do a few cosy, familiar things. Clean the coffee filter. Feed the Weevils. Stuff.'

'Good idea,' beamed Jack. 'And anyway, I don't trust you round sailors looking like that. I'll take Gwen. Much safer.'

He swept out. Gwen scowled at his back and followed him.

Ianto waited until they'd gone, and then slumped onto the table, auburn hair spilling out across the lacquer. 'Oh god,' he moaned.

CAPTAIN JACK IS FEELING BUOYANT

You can navigate Cardiff Bay by a succession of expensive follies with interesting names.

Beyond the Welsh Assembly Anti-Terrorist Barriers (erected at vast expense before someone pointed out that you could drive round them) but not quite as far as Cardiff International Heliport, lies the newly opened Cardiff International Ferryport.

Really it was just a patch of Docks not suitable for executive homes or freight due to poisonous mould. So someone had come up with the idea of running a highly subsidised ferry route to Ireland.

It took longer than going via Swansea, but was cheaper, and the ferry had been painted a cheerful shade of green. It had launched a couple of months earlier, with a lot of carbon-neutral fanfare.

When it had opened for business, Gwen had toyed with going. 'Ooh, it's just like the Eurostar,' Rhys had cooed mockingly, which had put an end to it.

And now here she was, standing at the terminal with Jack, watching the remains of the ferry dragged into the Docks by a tugboat.

The ferry had been a fine bit of 1970s engineering, kept afloat with Norwegian pride and a fresh lick of paint. Now it looked like a kicked tin can, strips of metal fluttering in the breeze like flags.

'Bloody hell,' breathed Gwen.

'I've been in worse,' said Jack, with a hint of professional pride. 'I've seen a World War Two mine rip a battleship apart like wet cardboard. Believe it or not, that ferry is still pretty much seaworthy. Ah, Norway, I salute you. Strong ships and even stronger sailors.'

'Right,' thought Gwen. 'I'll be spending the day interviewing stunned survivors in Portakabins while Jack's chatting up the crew. Marvellous.'

The ferry chugged past them, filthy water gushing from tears in the sides.

'No scorch marks,' said Gwen.

Jack shrugged. 'Not that unusual. Those are secondary explosions from the inside out.' He squinted. 'Yup. Good news. Definitely not claw marks.'

'You just don't want the paperwork,' teased Gwen.

They watched the ferry bump unsteadily into port.

'I don't want any of this,' he told her. 'Aliens are the new Health and Safety Nightmare. There are people in high places who are desperate to blame a Rift-related cause for this. It's more likely the boat just hit something – a World War Two mine's a World War Two mine you didn't see coming, whether or not it's drifted through the Rift. I don't like being scapegoated every time something goes wrong.'

'Aliens ate my homework?' Gwen laughed.

Jack laughed. 'What a brave new world. Now go and find some eyewitnesses to talk to.'

'What about Iantoya?' asked Gwen. 'Sure we don't need him?'

'Oh, he's best off at the Hub. Until he feels… you know… himself.'

'Jack Harkness, you are terrible. The poor lamb's got nothing to look forward to apart from filing, making the coffee and sexual harassment.'

'I know,' said Jack. 'I just want to surround him with familiar things.'

DORICE IS HER USUAL RED

Ianto had a quiet first morning as a woman. There was very little Rift activity, and only a few elderly tourists popped into the Tourist Information Centre that he manned above Torchwood. And then there was Dorice from the Shopping Centre, who dropped in with leaflets once a month. Dorice was, mostly in her own opinion, a right laugh. There was something about her that was a bit too red. He was never quite sure if it was her hair, her dress, her make-up or her nails, but the woman glowed.

He was surprised that he still couldn't work it out. He'd kind of hoped that, now he was a proper woman, he'd have some kind of X-Ray Fashion Vision that would allow him to solve the mystery of Dorice's redness. But no. There she was, leaving a huge lipstick mark on a cup of his excellent coffee, talking away, all hair and noise and redness. And still just as puzzlingly red. She was just a vaguely unattractive, slightly untidy, mildly overweight woman in her late forties.

But Dorice had talked, on and on, loudly and excitedly about developments and redevelopments in the Bay. Most of her talk was about the ferry crash, 'which is a shame, as I hope it catches on. I was dead excited at a trip to Minehead. Fancy that – me and Harry taking a mucky break to Butlin's. You know they've got their very own version of the Millennium Dome? Isn't that nice, especially as I never got to make it to the proper one. Did you dear?'

Oddly enough, Ianto had. One of his very first jobs at Torchwood had been at the Dome. To this day, whenever he saw a picture of it, he'd remember what was sealed underneath it, and shudder.

And now suddenly Dorice was at the door, and smiling. 'You do look lovely, dear. How long is my little bit of crumpet on holiday?'

'I'm sorry?'

'The nice lad they normally have running this place. Flirts like crazy, never serious though. You know the type. He's a very neat young boy. His hair is very carefully arranged.' She put the last two words in italics.

'Oh.' Ianto felt vaguely insulted. 'Not long, I hope. I'm just a temp.'

Dorice gave him a pitying look. 'Oh, I'm sorry to hear it, dear. Still, with that pair, I'm sure you'll go far.'

And then the door shut with a tinkle, and Ianto checked his watch. He realised for the first time how wrong it looked – a bulky man's watch around his tiny wrist. He was going to have to do something about it. Probably involving shopping. And Gwen. Hmm. She'd been a bit odd today – slightly like a cat defending her territory. Hmm. She'd not been like this around Tosh.

The thing was, Owen and Tosh would have been really handy right now. He'd admired Tosh – she was the only person in Torchwood who loved the place as much as he did. Something Ianto could only respect. She was quiet, polite, and thoughtful. Owen was just – well, he could be as nasty and bullying as he could be brilliant and charming. Even in those last months, when he'd hung around, all wrong and broken. Between them, they would know what to do.

He realised, with a certain dread, that he needed to pee again.

That was a horror show he still hadn't got used to. And these shoes were starting to hurt. Really hurt. He'd barely noticed them when he'd slipped them on this morning, but now it was like wearing a small pair of stilts made out of rusty chisels. Unsteadily, he hobbled off to the loo.

When he got back, Jack was there, leaning over his desk with a big grin that didn't quite meet his eyes.

He reached in the pockets of his greatcoat, and brought out two bottles of beer. 'I think we should drink to your first day.'

Ianto took them, and snapped them expertly open on the edge of the desk, passing one to Jack. They clinked bottles. Jack wiped it against his sleeve before drinking. 'I got them from Owen's medical fridge. He never got round to drinking them, and never got round to throwing them away. But I'd give it a wipe first – one of the livers is leaking.'

Ianto shuddered, and suddenly realised he no longer had sleeves. What was he supposed to do? He made a mental note to buy some tissues. One of those neat little packets. In the meantime, he made do with a leaflet about the new ferry service.

Jack leaned forward over the desk, as relaxed as a cat. 'Miss Ianto Jones! As your manager, I'm here to ask how your first day in your new body is going.'

'Fine, thank you,' said Ianto, not quite meeting his eyes.

'Settling in? No unexpected… wrinkles?'

Ianto shrugged. 'It's… strange. Actually, being a woman is a lot like being a man. Just unsettling. I'm like… You know when your mobile breaks and they give you a replacement that looks OK but isn't quite right? I'm that wrong phone.'

Jack placed a hand on Ianto's, and Ianto suddenly realised how small his hands were now. Jack's touch felt suddenly strange, and he drew back a little.

'Ianto Jones, I wouldn't know. Whenever my mobile breaks, you always get me a replacement that's exactly the same. That's what I love about you.'

'Yes, because you can't stand change. And don't use that word.' Ianto looked away. Jack had put the tiniest pause around the word 'love'. Beneath all that casual Jackness, he was trying to talk about feelings. Ianto had long suspected that Jack didn't really have feelings – just a succession of sugar rushes.

'OK. I just want you to know that this doesn't change things. I know you're still in there. We'll get you out.'

'Good.'

'And if you want to… after work…' A raised eyebrow and the Harkness grin.

'Oh god, no!' Ianto stepped back, aghast. 'No. Oh no! Not yet.'

'I'll take that as a maybe,' said Jack, unabashed. 'Look, we'll get you your body back. I've fired off a few emails to UNIT. Martha's on the case. And Gwen's been going through the archives. You're not unique – Torchwood's dealt with this kind of thing before. There's a protocol, some forms, even a pamphlet. The main thing is to try and find out if this is your body that's been altered somehow… or if there's been a body swap.'

'I had been wondering,' said Ianto. 'What if my body's still out there with this poor woman's mind in it?'

'Yeah – Gwen's set up a sweep on any CCTV in case your body turns up. Don't worry – it's all in hand. Just get on with living.'

'That's easy for you to say.'

Jack pulled a face. 'Sometimes it is. Sometimes it isn't.'

Ianto swigged down the rest of the beer and belched. Jack laughed. 'Oh, if I'd ever doubted it was you…'

'But you don't, do you?' Ianto wanted to know. Partly because Jack's trust was important to him, and partly because he didn't want to wake up in a cell.

Again, the reassuring touch, the smile, but the strange look in Jack's eyes. 'No. I miss the old you – but I'll have to get used to the new one.'

There was a silence between them. An awkward one. Ianto put his bottle neatly in the recycling.

Jack clapped his hands and put on some fresh cheer. 'What say we go out tonight? There's a town out there just waiting to be painted red.'

Ianto shook his head and swung off the desk. 'Not tonight. I know you'll laugh, but I've got a sudden urge to go home, run a bath and light a lot of candles.' Truly, I just don't want to be around you.

Jack held his glance. He knows I'm lying, thought Ianto. But he nodded, just slightly.

At just the right moment, Gwen came in. 'Jack! Andy's been on the phone. Says there's a body in a restaurant that's right up your street.'

'A body, eh?' Impressed, Jack swung his legs off the desk and bounded into action. 'Your police friend's really getting to know my tastes. Sometimes, I don't know whether to jump him or wipe his memory.'

'Both,' whispered Gwen to Ianto.

Jack clapped his hands together. 'Let's head out. Ianto – you up for a body?'

Ianto considered. 'OK. But first I've got to pee again.'

PAMELA'S SUDDENLY SHORTER

Torchwood operative
instructions for
When You Discover You're Not
Who You Thought You Were.
(Last revised 1958)

There are five classic stages to body dislocation and misplacement.

STAGE I: Disbelief, fear and horror

Relax, this is the worst bit. Especially if your consciousness has been transplanted into a non-terrestrial organism, potentially with a superfluity of limbs. The good news is, if you're reading this, you're over the worst of it – if your mind couldn't cope with the alien signal inputs, then it'd all be over by now. Instead, don't worry.

You're going to be fine.

From the Torchwood Archives

GWEN IS WEARING CORPSE

The skeleton sat looking out over Cardiff Bay, its hand resting on a glass of champagne which was still fizzing slightly.

'Oh yes, definitely one for us,' Jack was assuring the restaurant's owner. Gwen was dividing her attention between the corpse and Ianto.

She was just about used to Ianto being a woman. Well, more or less. The weird thing was it was exactly, completely Ianto. Self-deprecating, quietly ironic, bashful. Only in the body of a woman who looked like she'd stepped from the set of Hotel Babylon.

Ianto was standing, staring at the body, completely entranced. His head was on one side, his mouth slack with unbecoming surprise. 'Um,' Ianto said, using lips that had clearly never said anything uncertain before in their lives. 'This is quite a new thing.' He bent over the table to examine something.

Gwen caught the manager checking out Ianto's magnificent arse. Ah well, she thought. And she'd got used to being the pretty one. Poor Ianto – she wondered if he realised the effect he was having on men. Knowing him, probably not. But Gwen was going to have to have a little word about posture. He still moved like a Valleys Boy in a new suit, stiff, slightly afraid, and ever so slightly ungainly. Plus he kept sticking his arse in the air like a duck bobbing for food. It was like presenting a target to the entire restaurant staff. Still, Gwen guessed it distracted everyone, just slightly, from the enormous lump of skeleton sat at the table.

She wondered how Jack was feeling about Ianto. Was he being all sympathetic and reasonable, or just leaping on the poor lamb? She glanced briefly at Jack. He was watching Ianto and grinning. This was just one long sexy party for Jack, she decided.

Gwen went over to the counter where they kept the CCTV and started spooling through it. She'd called Rhys on the way to the restaurant, and tried explaining it all to him, but she'd got no further than 'Ianto's now a woman. Ianto. The quiet man who makes the coffee. No. Not in that sense. He's not a trans-anything. He just came into work this morning as a woman. Yes. No! Of course I haven't checked! No, Rhys, it's a completely different body. I absolutely assure you he's not tucked it up. Well, I guess so. Look- No, look, the point is that he's gorgeous and I- Shut up. Listen- Well, yes I know about your Canadian cousin. It's not like that at all.'

The CCTV bore out the manager's story in time-lapse. Crowded lunchtime in a Cardiff restaurant. Lots of business. Only a few empty tables. People came and went. 3pm: the restaurant started tidying up after lunch. 3.17pm: between one frame and the next, the skeleton appeared. 3.18pm: one of the waiters noticed, and the screaming begins.

Gwen pocketed the disc and went over to the table.

Jack was looking at the skeleton, and standing closer to Ianto than he'd ever stood before. He smiled at Gwen briefly, and then looked back at the corpse. 'It's a young skeleton,' he said.

'How can you tell?' asked Ianto. Gwen suddenly realised that he really, really missed having pockets. His hands were patting the top of his skirt nervously. It wasn't an attractive look.

'Calcium deposits?' put in Gwen.

Jack shook his head and pointed to the body. 'It's the clothes – they're very new, they're trendy without being expensive. We can bother with the scanners in a bit, but I'm going to bet this was a young man.'

'Out on a date,' Gwen put in. 'The table's set for two, and he's wearing his finest pulling gear. White shirt for clubbing, stripy shirt for a date. Those are the rules.'

'Oh those rules,' sighed Jack. 'What did the CCTV tell us?'

'Middle of the afternoon. Blink and he's there. But the look of the table suggests he's been there hours.'

Ianto checked a clipboard, happily. 'Table's got a good view.'

Jack nodded. 'See if he's got a wallet or a phone would you, Gwen?'

Gwen bent over and started rifling through the pockets,

Ianto had spotted something. 'There's lipstick on this coffee cup!' observed Ianto.

'Excellent work, Ms Jones,' said Jack.

Gwen sighed, and tried to feel inside the jacket without touching the ribcage or retching. She managed to undo one of the buttons and was just edging her hand in when the body moved slightly and – oh god – she touched it, then jerked back as the body moved. It fell forward and just hit the table and carried on going, and she yelled and shut her eyes.

When she opened them again, she was covered in dust. There was no sign of the skeleton, just a pile of clothes. She gagged.

'I just touched it and...'

Ianto shook his gorgeous head disapprovingly, and bent over the body. 'Well, here's the mobile,' he said.

Gwen started to brush herself down. 'Honestly, I just...'

Jack tutted. 'Complete cellular exhaustion. The only thing holding those molecules together was boredom. Just a tiny nudge and...'

Ianto smiled. 'Aw, Gwen, it's made such a mess of your nice trousers.'

Gwen laughed. 'Look at Ianto Jones, criticising my clothes! Fancy that – your first bitchy comment. Welcome to the sisterhood.'

Jack looked up from sweeping some dust into an envelope. 'You two aren't going to gang up on me, are you?'

Gwen's mobile rang. Inevitably Rhys. No matter how many times she said 'Please don't call me at work unless another starliner lands in The Hayes, or there's a new *Heat* with Gavin or Charl looking fat.'

'Hello, lover!' he said. 'What's up? Apart from Ianto's cup size.'

Gwen stepped out onto the balcony. It was cold and windy, and she watched the wind blow vital crime-scene evidence off her and into the Bay. Ah well. 'Nothing much. I'm covered in bits of corpse.'

'Eugh!' there was a pause. 'I was eating a doughnut,' said Rhys reproachfully.

'I *knew* you were cheating,' Gwen smiled. Rhys was on another semi-diet, which gave Gwen hours of innocent pleasure.

'No... not really. Pastries left over after a meeting. Stolen food doesn't count.'

'Really?'

'You've always said so. Anyway, corpse?'

'Yeah.' Gwen did a little relationship maths – how much could she tell him against how much would it make her feel better. 'Yeah. Skeleton turned up at a table-for-two.'

'You are kidding! Classy!' Rhys sounded worryingly enthusiastic. 'Where?'

'You'll never believe it – Abalone's,' said Gwen.

Rhys laughed. 'Wouldn't be seen dead in there!'

'Well quite,' said Gwen. 'Poor bugger seemed to be on a date.'

'Abalone's. What a way to go. It's only one up from keeling over at the Chinese Buffet. What'll you tell the relatives? Died of shame?'

'Ah,' said Gwen. 'We're still working out who he is. You see, I touched him and he… well, exploded over me…'

There was a dangerous pause, in which Rhys had the chance to say something reassuring. Instead: 'So you're seriously wearing skellington?' Rhys was really amused. More amused than when Gwen had trodden in dog turd. Wearing flip-flops. 'Well, mind you have a shower before tonight – we're going round to Darren and Sian's. They've got a new pet.'

'What did they choose?' Knowing them it was going to be something fluffy and low maintenance. Their ideal pet would be a spider plant that could purr.

Another laugh from Rhys. 'A rat.'

Gwen squeaked. 'Oh this is the best day ever.'

PATRICK MATTHEWS IS NOT DEAD

Gwen scurried back into Torchwood. She'd nipped out for a sandwich and got soaked. She'd needed a break from combing through interviews with ferry passengers and CCTV from the bar. She'd been hoping to come back refreshed. Instead her teeth were chattering.

And there was Ianto. Sat at a desk, looking annoyingly perfect, not a hair out of place.

'You bloody cow,' laughed Gwen, dumping her bag on the desk. 'How do you do it? You look… You're not even wearing make-up.'

Ianto shrugged. 'It's getting weird, isn't it? It's like this body can only be pretty.' He pointed to the hair. 'And the hair! It just naturally… bounces into place. I've not even moisturised. This'll take some getting used to.'

'Hey, ladies!' Jack bounded into the office, laying a fond hand on Ianto's shoulder. I bet they're at it like rabbits, thought Gwen. Jack picked up a leaflet on caravanning in the Gower and then favoured them with a wide grin. 'Ianto Jones – looking amazing. Gwen Cooper – looking damp. Keep it up troops!' They followed him through into Owen's old medical area, where what remains they'd salvaged lay in an untidy heap on a slab.

'I have news about our corpse,' said Ianto. 'His wallet says he's Patrick Matthews. He checks up as living in Adamstown. He's 25. And he's still alive.'

'Really?' Jack looked pleased.

Ianto nodded. 'I went over to his flat. He answered the door. Oddly, I didn't have to think of a cover story. He seemed perfectly happy to chat.' With those knockers, I bet he bloody did, thought Gwen. 'Nice bloke, really,' Ianto went on. 'Works in Chippie Alley, moved from Neath. Got a nice car. Very friendly. Even gave me his mobile number – but told me it wasn't working. He was off to get a new one, which was why I'd caught him in. Not at all dead in any way.'

'Ah.' Jack held up the corpse's phone. 'I have a theory. Two copies of the same mobile can't function on the same network. You'd need a degree in temporal engineering and a soldering iron to get around it. Dusty the Corpse is from the future.'

Ianto coughed, gently. 'And there's more. I rang the restaurant. Patrick Matthews has booked a table for Saturday.'

Jack wore an expression which on any other man would have been embarrassed. 'Tricky. Tricky.' He spread his hands out in a really big shrug. 'We used to hate stuff like this at the Time Agency. We'd have seminars. Really boring seminars. And don't even get me started on the flowcharts.'

'Jack!' Gwen didn't quite shout. 'What do we do? Can we stop this?'

Jack's look turned shifty. 'Maybe. Maybe not. Perhaps he does die. Perhaps not. That's the problem. He dies in the future, his corpse turns up here. But if we prevent him from dying – what happens? It's a massive ticking paradox inches away from a colossal space-time rift.'

'Are you saying we do nothing?'

'Not... nothing. I'm just saying that we might not be able to do anything. There's two ways of looking at it. And one of them argues that we can spend the rest of the week trying to save Patrick Matthews – and somehow, he'll still die. Do we really want to spend the next week in one of those films about doomed teenagers who die with hilarious consequences? Kind of hoped we were classier than that.'

Gwen thought about it. Rhys liked *Final Destination* way more than she did. That was a fact. Her left shoe was more wet than her right one. That was also a fact. You couldn't even go out for a meal in Cardiff these days without causing a space-time paradox. Third fact. Hmm. She glanced at her watch. Not even 7pm. This was turning into another long day.

'Right.' Ianto's voice was soft and echoed across the Hub. 'We've got a week to work out who's going to kill him. Failing that, we just turn up on the night.'

Jack started to open his mouth to argue, but Ianto carried on speaking. 'It's the least we can do. Maybe it's fated that he'll die. But maybe we can find the killer. What does it say about that on your flowcharts?'

Jack spread out his hands helplessly, and for a second looked like a farmboy with a missing cow. 'To be honest, we never got to the end of the flowcharts. They were really big, the print was very small, and most of us were bombed by that point. See what you can find out about him, I guess.'

Later Jack sauntered over to Gwen's desk. They'd spent the last few minutes pretty much not making eye contact. 'So,' he said, 'are we going to have a row about this?'

'I dunno, Jack,' she said. 'I've got a million things on, I'm soaking wet, and I just want to get home, shower and put some warm, dry clothes on.' She managed a weak smile. 'But doing nothing feels… wrong. I want to try.'

'Really?' Jack was looking directly at her, nearly smiling. 'Potential paradoxes are really, really bad. You behave nicely around them, and the universe doesn't end. Trust me – I've spent chunks of the last century not bumping into myself. You get a knack for how to behave around paradoxes. Approach them like male models – very carefully and only from behind.

If we can save him, then we will. But I can't have you following your heart on this one. It'll go horribly, horribly wrong. I need to rely on you to do the right thing.' His smile suddenly flickered on. He sipped his coffee. 'Is it me, or has Ianto's coffee got better since he's a woman?'

And, with that little misdirection, he was gone, bounding back to his desk.

That was bloody useless, thought Gwen, miserably. A few reassuring words, a bit of sexy banter, a lot of *que sera sera*. She looked back at the photo of Patrick Matthews floating across her screen. According to his Facebook status, he was booking a holiday. Bloody hell, thought Gwen.

EMMA WEBSTER IS ATTENDING SPEED-DATING IN THE BAY

Hi, I'm Ross. I'm with the
No. Too old.

Hi, I'm Terry. I'm
God, those teeth.

Hi, I'm Roger. By name and
Tosser.

Evening, gorgeous. I'm
There is not enough vodka in the world.

Actually. I'm fed up of all of them. Can you make them go away?

An hour later the phone call came in.
'A bar full of skeletons?' said Jack.

TOMBOLA'S IS THE IDEAL VENUE FOR YOUR NEXT PARTY

Tombola's was one of those places. It was hard to see why anyone would go there for a drink unless it was for a reason. It wasn't a bar you'd drop in on. The brewery were baffled. Clearly, the architect had put a lot of work in, and the décor was very nice – quite modern, quite classy, quite solid wood and cosy bunk beds. The beers were nice, the food wasn't bad, the music wasn't offensive. It was all very safe and ordinary – and the folk of Cardiff avoided it like the plague. Which meant it was easy to book it for a function – so it was popular with book groups, societies, and so on.

It had needlessly roped off an area for speed-dating. The area was full of corpses. All dressed up. All ready to go. All dead.

'Well, they're all men. I think we're looking for a woman.' Jack smiled. 'Forget Mister Right – we're looking for Miss Wrong.' He stuck his hands on his hips and grinned broadly.

Jack Harkness, thought Gwen, I love you, but sometimes, you can be very hard work.

An hour later and they'd managed to collect twelve wallets and mobiles and only destroyed two bodies. Miraculously, Ianto had managed to avoid getting any of the dust on him. Whereas Gwen was caked in dead people. She was mentally rehearsing comebacks for any witty comments that Rhys might manage when she finally staggered in. But that wasn't going to be for a long time.

Ianto confirmed there wasn't any CCTV footage. 'But, interesting development – the place was booked for speed-dating. And, as far as anyone can tell, this was it. The bar staff agree that everything was going on very much as normal, and then… all of a sudden… this.'

'Yeah, but that's stupid,' said Gwen, a little harsher than she'd intended. 'There are twelve men here. Where are the women? You don't just get one woman – it's normally a group. Fuelled on zambuca and desperation.'

Ianto reached into a large pink rucksack and pulled out a scanner which he ran over each of the bodies. 'Nothing,' he said. 'No abnormal emissions, no radiation traces. Slightly elevated static electricity.'

'Really?' said Jack.

'Yes. Twenty-three per cent. Same as over the rest of town.'

'Oh.'

'Right. This is peculiar.' Ianto was scanning the room. He shrugged, which pushed back the straps on his shoulders. 'No… something's odd here. Each skeleton… it's… perfect. Full set of teeth. No bones broken. Great posture. No fillings.'

Gwen laughed. 'Twelve Welsh men without a single filling?'

The skeletons sat at various tables across the room, all in postures of polite attention.

'So,' said Jack slowly. 'Apart from the mysteriously vanishing women, someone is taking men, making them physically perfect, then killing them?'

'Don't forget about sending the odd one back through time,' put in Ianto.

'Marvellous.'

BREN IS VERY PRECISE

It had been a long, long night, thought Ianto, but he had one thing more to do.

He was walking down St Mary Street. It was raining, but Cardiff was in full party mood. Tight hunting packs of single men, pumped arms and white shirts, strode past. Little groups of women stood queuing sulkily outside clubs. Everywhere were bouncers, flyer girls, and police just, you know, waiting.

And it was freezing. Last time he was out on the lash he'd been wearing a duffle coat. Now all he had to keep the elements at bay was a mini-skirt, a pair of tights and a light denim jacket. The rain was slicing through him. He was dying with each step.

Around him were girls wearing less and laughing more.

A gust of icy breeze lifted his skirt, and he heard some men across the street make a 'Woooooo!' noise. He glanced across at them, and they barked back.

Ianto cursed under his breath and carried on walking. 'Lovely night for a spot of MurderRape.' He got stopped briefly by an enormous queue outside a club. He stood there for a bit, trying not to jostle, sensing the ogling glances of the men, and the strange, jealous glares of the women.

A meaty hand landed on his arm. 'Aw, not going home already, luv, are we?' A boy's voice, rough and slurred, sweet with beer, too close to his ear.

Ianto nodded. 'I've got a boyfriend, sorry,' he said quickly, and carried on walking.

All around him was noise and screaming, and empty glass bottles and rain, and the greasy smell of kebabs and piss. By the time he found the chip shop he was looking for, he was fed up and dripping, and he pushed gratefully inside, past a sign advertising curry with half and half. The shop stank of salt and vinegar and comfort. He shivered and made his way through the quiet crowd to the counter.

The shop was busy, as ever, the windows fogged up – couples sharing chips and sauce on the tiny lean-to formica counters, tight huddles of lads arguing over their orders, quiet groups of drunk girls, nudging and waiting and texting and stabbing at their chips with dainty mini-forks. And just one tiny little old lady behind the counter doing everything. Bren was a Cardiff institution, and a personal hero of Ianto's – she was more organised and placid than he was. He just saved the world on a regular basis – but she kept order in St Mary Street on a party night. To the best of his knowledge, no one had ever had it large in Brenda's.

She barely peered at him through her enormous fishbowl spectacles, waiting patiently for his order.

'Aw, hello, Bren,' said Ianto, cheered to see a familiar face, 'How are you?'

She fixed him with a sudden razor gaze. 'I don't know you, dear,' she said, quite certain of it.

'No, sorry,' said Ianto, slightly crestfallen. 'I'm actually looking for Patrick.'

Bren held his gaze ever so firmly. 'He's out the back, luv, doing the batter.' She leant back and raised her voice delicately. 'Lady for you, Pat.' And then Ianto was swept aside in favour of Vimto and a saveloy.

Patrick emerged, puzzled and then blinking happily. For a

dead man he was in great health. He was tall and broad, with a grinning rugby-build that showed no signs of going to seed. He was wearing an old T-shirt, a little chef's hat and an apron covered in flour. 'It's you – funny name girl. Er, Ianto, isn't it?' he said. 'Still checking up on me? Come through.'

He lifted the heavy formica counter, and Ianto stepped through into another world, past Tupperware, a smell of hot oil and jars of pickled eggs, and a slowly spinning kebab.

'Sorry if I don't shake your hand, but I'm breading fish,' Patrick explained, moving to a table and working quickly. 'What brings you here? Girls' night out?'

Ianto looked baffled and then remembered. 'Oh, no. No. Well, a bit, but just a quiet drink with friends. Tombola's,' he put in quietly as an extra detail. No reaction. 'Although we nearly went to Abalone's.'

Patrick smirked at that and carried on quietly, expertly mixing up a batch of batter. 'Abalone's, eh? What would you think if I took you on a date there?' His smile was sly.

Oh. Oh god, he fancies me. Ianto thought of something smart to say or do, and instead gave a little snorty giggle. With horror, he noticed a tiny fleck of snot land in the batter, but realised that Patrick was looking away. 'Er… well… er…'

Patrick met his gaze and smiled. 'Look, I'll be truthful. You're a pretty girl. And I was supposed to be going speed-dating there. They do a deal when you sign up – you book a table in advance for the Saturday night at a discount. So if I met someone nice, I could take them there.'

'I see,' said Ianto, not seeing at all. 'And?'

'Well,' said Patrick. 'I just wondered – is it a naff place to take a date?'

'Oh,' said Ianto, distracted into considering it seriously. 'Well, it depends. Now me, I love a salad bar. Especially one with a sneeze guard.'

'So that's a yes?' asked Patrick, washing his hands in the sink.

He was smiling with a natural confidence that Ianto had never really had.

'What?'

'God, why do the pretty ones always make a meal out of it? Look, gorgeous, I'm saying screw the speed-dating. Why don't I just take you to Abalone's, sneeze guard and all?'

Oh dear. He's asking me out on a date. Right. What? But... What do I do about this? If I go, perhaps I'll save his life. Or break the space-time continuum. Or end up pregnant. That's a whole new risk. What would Jack do? Ianto thought hard. And realised that Jack would barely have glanced at Patrick's wicked grin and blue eyes before having him up against the gherkins.

I need a better role model, thought Ianto glumly.

'OK,' said Ianto, slowly. 'Firstly, why are you asking me out, please?'

Patrick wiped his big hands down on his apron. 'Oh come on, Ianto. When you walked in here it wasn't to watch me batter a sausage.' He laid a hand on Ianto's shoulder and drew close. 'Or was it...?'

'Well,' began Ianto, 'actually, it was to save your life.'

Patrick took it as a joke and leaned in closer. He was wearing quite a nice scent, Ianto decided. 'Really? You're my saviour, are you?'

'Oh yes,' said Ianto, suddenly noticing how warm a fish and chip shop was. 'Uh, yes. Seriously. I didn't knock on your door by accident today. I was looking out for you.'

'My guardian angel?'

'Sort of,' said Ianto. 'I'm slightly psychic, see, and I saw you out the other night, and I had a premonition.' He rolled the last word like a preacher.

Patrick laughed heartily, and clapped his giant hands on Ianto's shoulders, drawing him into a big, easy hug. 'Oh you are precious and funny.'

He pecked the side of Ianto's cheek and then drew back. 'So, gorgeous, you want to be around me and watch over me? Is that it?' He grinned a big grin and then kissed Ianto again, this time on the lips. Ianto discovered two entirely new things about being a woman.

Patrick leaned back, and smiled at Ianto. 'OK then. If I survive till the end of the week, we'll go to Abalone's. How about that, angel?'

Ianto was quite distracted for a second, but eventually replied. 'Yes. Right then. So long as I'm just saving your life. If that's all right?'

Patrick laughed. 'It's quite all right. You know, you aren't like the other WAGs we get in here. You're very shy. It's rather sweet.'

He was about to kiss Ianto again, but they were interrupted by Bren bustling loudly down the corridor. 'Pat, luv, there are customers who need to tuck into a good mutton pie. I can't have you out here all night handling the fish.' Bren gave Ianto the briefest of glances.

'Yes, Nan,' said Patrick, cowed just a bit, but also smirking. 'Come on,' he said to Ianto, leading him back to the counter and holding it up like a wedding arch. 'See you Saturday, unless you feel the sudden need to save my life first.'

His hand brushed against Ianto's skirt and then he went over to heat up some pies, giving Ianto an enormous wink.

Ianto watched Patrick's back as he worked and realised that, for the first time, he was actually enjoying being a woman. Suddenly hungry, he turned to Bren. 'Can I have some chips after all?'

Without looking up Bren got to work. 'Small chips, is it?' she said. '1.20 thanks, love.'

As Ianto walked out, he was oblivious to the two flour handprints over the back of his skirt.

Back out in the rain, he took three steps, trying to eat the chips and shield them from the weather. Steam rose from them, wafting around in the downpour. They didn't taste of much, other than hot, but somehow they comforted him. A crowd of blokes edged past, their eyes all over him. Someone grabbed his arse, and he flinched and forced himself to move on. If only you bloody knew, he thought.

Later, he'd ask Gwen how she coped with an evening of constant ogling. She'd grin and say, 'Well, most of the time, I was all padded up in my lovely copper's outfit. That tends to soften the curves a bit. You still get a bit of chat, mind, but it's all "awright luv?" banter. Honestly, if I'm lucky, someone'll tell me that they'll come quietly. You know. Clever. But not so bad.'

Yeah, Ianto would say, but what about when she was out... properly? And Gwen would shrug and grin. 'I gave as good as I got.' And Ianto didn't doubt it for a second.

But for the moment there was just the chips and the rain. Ianto pressed on, past the bright lights of the last shop open selling cigarettes in Cardiff. One foot in front of the other.

These bloody, bloody shoes. I am never doing this again. And definitely never sober.

The chips were cold and damp. The rain was in everything.

I am completely soaked and sodden. I will never be warm and dry. I absolutely hate being a woman.

Ianto saw something in the street ahead, a figure standing in the shadows by the scaffolding. Something really quite—

Oh is that a cab?

Ianto rushed towards the flickering amber light sluicing down the road. He knew that around him a mini-stampede of drunk boys and desperate girls were all lurching towards the cab. But Ianto knew that he needed it more than anyone else. Screw the shoes, he was going to get it.

He got his hand on the door and was met by the baleful, seen-it-all gaze of the cabbie. 'You going to be sick?' asked the voice.

'Stone-cold sober,' promised Ianto. The door clicked open and he climbed gratefully in.

'There's a charge for sick, you know. And I hate having to scrub the back out. Why they can't do it in a bag, I dunno. Bloody animals.'

And the cab puttered away, taking Ianto home through the storm. He sat there, hands scrunched round his bag of damp chips, thinking back to what he'd seen on the street just before he'd noticed the cab, with all its amber promise of home and central heating and towels. Because, as he'd been waving his hands at the cab, there'd been a man standing just ahead of him in the street. The man had been standing in the shadows of some scaffolding by the market. He'd just been standing there, looking at Ianto. It hadn't been a look of lust, desire or even disgust. The look had been one of shock, or fear. Like he'd seen a ghost.

Ianto unwrapped the dead bag of chips and stared at them. Am I a ghost?

Standing there in the rain, watching the taxi drive off, Ross Kielty couldn't believe what he'd just seen.

Everyone in Cardiff slept badly that night.

GWEN IS AWAKE FIRST

Gwen lay in bed, killing time before the alarm by staring at the back of Rhys's head.

'I know what you're doing, you know,' mumbled Rhys without moving. 'Stop it.'

'Stop what?' Gwen was all innocence.

'You are staring at the back of my head. I can tell.'

'How?'

'Burning sensation. Will you be happy if I get a bald spot? I don't think so.'

'Oh, no worries about that. Fine head of hair. Few bits of grey, though. Quite a few.'

'No way. We Williamses don't go grey.'

'Awwww, Rhys. It's fine – get used to going grey. There's no harm in a bit of grey. It's… distinguished.'

'I. Am. Not. Grey.'

'Of course you're not, love. Now, hurry up and storm off and make us some tea.'

'Not until you admit that I've not got grey hair.'

There was a click, and then Gwen leaned over him holding up her camera phone jubilantly.

'Yes. I think it's called salt-and-pepper. See?'

'That's just bad light.'

Rhys pulled the covers over his head.
'Just go and make the tea.'

IANTO IS STAYING IN BED

Ianto Jones had a difficult second day as a woman. It started with waking up from dreams of dark, cold water and then with a shock, as though he'd fallen, spread out in his bed. And he'd forgotten, for the first few seconds, stretching out to touch the radio alarm, seeing his long, slender arm – seeing it but not noticing it.

And then he'd remembered.

Normally, Ianto Jones would wake up, swing his legs out of the bed, slope off for a pee and a shower and be out of the flat in twenty minutes. He'd have laid out his suit and shirt the night before, his lunch waiting in a Tupperware box in the fridge. It was order and a system, and he was proud of it.

But that was the old Ianto Jones. The new Ianto Jones sat in bed, wrapped in a duvet, listening to the radio babble away, staring out of the window. He didn't even have much of a view, but he didn't really know what else to do. He just watched the barren tops of three trees sway about in the wind like empty flagpoles.

Nearly an hour passed by. He went and stood in the shower, staring at the mirror as it steamed up and hid his new body from view. And he stood there feeling invisible and warm and hidden until he felt guilty about using that much hot water. And then he got out of the shower and dried quickly before the mirror cleared. Then he crawled back into the warmth of the duvet.

He heard the click of the door, and ignored it. He knew it was Jack standing there in his bedroom doorway, looking at him.

Neither of them spoke for a bit. Then Ianto managed, 'I never gave you a key.'

'And I never really needed one, but the gesture would have been nice.'

'Ah well.' Ianto heard Jack move across the room and felt him settle on the bed next to him.

'Well, here am I,' said Jack, 'in the bedroom of a beautiful, naked Torchwood operative. Anything could happen.'

'You realise the only word I heard was "beautiful"?'

'I realise. I'm checking that you're OK.'

'What do you think?'

'I dunno.' Jack nodded. 'You never even considered getting somewhere in Grangetown with a view?'

'There are no views in Grangetown.'

'Good point.' Jack leaned in and wrapped a big arm around the duvet and Ianto, drawing them both in. Ianto let himself be folded up, marvelling at how much wet hair he had.

'I miss you, you know,' said Jack.

Ianto laughed. 'I miss me.'

'But you're still in there.'

'Am I? It feels less and less like me. This body just gets more and more perfect. I can almost sense it – it hates me. I don't belong inside it. I'm the wrong soul in the driving seat.' He looked across at Jack.

'If the real owner is somewhere out there in your body, she's not shown up. Nothing.'

'It's at times like this,' sighed Ianto, 'we need Tosh.'

'Oh yeah,' said Jack.

'Apart from the whole science bit, she had some great jackets.'

'Oh yeah,' said Jack. He stood up and reached out his hand. Ianto took it. 'Come on, Miss Jones. Let's put on some clothes and face the day.'

EMMA WEBSTER IS PLOTTING REVENGE

It was on Tuesday that Vile Kate finally noticed the change in Emma. It had taken her a day longer than everyone else.

Kate had been in one of Her Meetings. These went on for a long time, were supposedly very difficult, and she pretended she found them A Terrible Chore, while at the same time dropping simpering hints about how Vital she was to the organisation, and how close she was to all the powerful people. When Kate walked in, she was talking to Arwel, the new researcher. 'Honestly, she put down her Blackberry and gave me a big hug and told me how nice this perfume was. Do you like it? It's very similar to something Posh wears.'

And then Kate looked at Emma. And noticed her. New, slim, gorgeous, perfect Emma. And her mouth formed a lovely little 'oh' and a frown. And for a glorious instant she looked like a sex doll. Emma grinned. Kate snapped on a warm smile. 'Oh, Emma lovely, look at you! It's so nice to see you making an effort in the office!' She turned around to her colleagues with a fond look that said 'See, everyone, what she can do when she tries!' and settled down to work.

To Emma's horror, everyone nodded at that.

I can give her cancer.

What?

I can give her cancer. Incurable, slow, painful cancer that burns away more steadily than your hate.

Emma's head flooded with a sudden, delicious view of Vile Kate, sat at her desk, weeping and clutching clumps of hair that had fallen out.

No.

Really? Too much? Not even for a couple of weeks? How about a bit of a scare? Go on, the tiniest non-malignant lump. But, you know, worrying enough that they'll chop off her boobs. Go on…

Emma shut her eyes and felt dizzy. She breathed in deeply and then out. And felt the red mist gently float away.

No. I hate her. But I don't really know her. I don't want to… maybe later. Is there anything small you can do?

Well, she's had work done. Those boobs aren't real, and her lips have had a bit of plumping. I can soon sort that out.

Really? Oh that's brilliant.

And… I can make her fat.

Emma giggled, remembering all the little comments about struggling to bring up bebbies and maintain her figure.

Do it.

Nice one! I think you'll love the results. And then some day you can dance on her grave while her fat children watch.

Emma smiled warmly and truly. A few minutes later some of the girls asked if she wanted to join them for lunch for the first time in ages. 'You look really… confident,' said one. And Emma beamed.

'So how are you?' asked Sharon. 'We're all dead impressed with your makeover. How are you feeling?'

Emma watched Kate walking over to the salad bar, laughing with one of the Divisional Sales Managers while ostentatiously picking out a few green leaves. 'Perfect,' she said.

IANTO TRIES BEIGE

Gwen walked along the wharf, trying to ignore how cold and wet it was. There are mornings when Cardiff Bay looks like Venice Beach, and there are mornings when it looks like Norway. Today was not one of the better ones, and sheets of rain lashed across the decking outside Torchwood. Gwen had already dropped her keys as she locked up the car and, added to that, a mild hangover refused to be ignored. Last night had been a late one, but she'd finally made it to Darren and Sian's before Rhys drank all the wine. It was surprisingly fun, and the rat almost cute, even though she'd insisted Rhys wash his hands the moment they'd got home. Gawd, when had she drunk so much wine? She tried to clear her head. It felt like she hadn't slept at all. The weekend seemed a long way away.

She let herself into the Tourist Information entrance to Torchwood and shivered. Despite living in Cardiff for years, Gwen had never bought an umbrella. It always struck her as giving in. Anyway, she hadn't been allowed them on long nights on police duty, and it seemed silly to get her own when Rhys had a ridiculous golfing one with a daft corporate logo.

It was an odd day. Ianto was late for work. When he finally arrived, he seemed fine, bustling around, very much his old self. But every now and then, Gwen thought she caught a look of utter misery on his face. Plus, he was wearing a really inadvisable beige trouser suit.

'I've been shopping on the way in,' he explained. 'Everything so far has been Lisa's. But I figured it's a bit… you know…'

'Creepy?' Gwen was quietly appalled.

Ianto nodded. 'Yeah. Dead girlfriend's clothes. I know. But I still had some of her stuff, and I figured… well, she's the woman I know the most, really. Well, that's not true. There's also my mother. But, firstly, it's just wrong, and secondly, floral print.' He put on a brave smile, showing off perfect teeth. 'Anyway, I spotted this on the way in. It feels a bit more… me.'

Gwen nodded, kindly. 'Yes. Very nice.'

Jack wandered past. 'Ianto. Beige. No.' He vanished into his office.

Ianto sighed. 'Were you being polite?'

'No, no. No. Well. A little,' she admitted.

'OK. It's so hard being… you know… A woman. I thought I was doing OK, but the shopping is just…'

'Hard?'

'Yes. And expensive. Jack really doesn't give you a clothing allowance?'

'No.'

'Right. And I can't take this back – I've already got Weevil blood on the cuff, and that's a stain that never lifts.' He gave her a look, and suddenly Gwen saw the old Ianto shining out of this new body – all Valleys Boy mildly confused by the world.

'We'll go shopping. Promise. Or get Jack to take you.'

'Um.'

'Is everything… OK… between the two of you?' Gwen asked.

'Not really. He's fine… you know. But at the same time, I think he still worries that I might not be Ianto. And I can't talk to anyone else about it. Not my friends, not my family. How do I explain? I've told my neighbours I'm flat-sitting while I'm…

he's on holiday. If you get what I mean. But they're not going to believe that for ever. It's all so bloody… and I can't talk to anyone. You're… Gwen… you're it.'

Christ, Ianto's unspooling, thought Gwen. Poor lamb.

'Come on, Ianto. Jack will get you your old body back. Don't give up. Any luck with the memory pill?'

Ianto shook his head, his long, beautiful hair following lazily, like it was in a shampoo commercial. 'No, not really. I can suddenly quote all of *Under Milk Wood* and vividly recall having my wisdom teeth out. But nothing useful.'

'Never mind. Tomorrow we're bunking off. You'll love shopping.'

'Thank you, Gwen.'

Don't mention it, thought Gwen, feeling a lot better.

Ianto had combed through Patrick's Facebook profile and failed to come up with any coherent theories on who might want to kill him, or any brushes he might have had with alien technology. He and Gwen had been delighted to find a picture of Patrick running across a beach in speedos, but that was about it.

Jack was kept fairly busy dealing with reports of atmospheric disturbances around the city. Apparently static electricity was up by a quarter now, which Jack seemed to find curiously amusing.

Gwen was occupied assuring a rather weasel-like Assembly liaison that the Rift honestly had had nothing to do with the ferry crash in the Bay. It was one of those things – slightly mysterious, which meant that Torchwood had to be all over it. But she couldn't quite work out what to do really, other than interview the survivors, who all seemed a bit dazed and not very communicative. But then, most of them had either hypothermia or concussion so it wasn't really that surprising. As far as she could tell, the ferry had started taking on water just outside the Bay, listed alarmingly, but had made it into dock.

Even Jack's theory of a mine seemed off – Gwen had examined the hull, and couldn't find any evidence of an explosion. So: more talking to gruff Norwegians and dazed people who'd been on a hen night.

EMMA WEBSTER IS HAVING IT MEDIUM

Emma Webster logged off from her computer and got ready to go home. She was glowing but exhausted. Who knew being this beautiful would be so tiring? She acknowledged a couple of friendly nods from the boy totty in sales as they left for the day. Tiring, yes, but worth it.

The last couple of days had been a whirlwind. Previously, her life had been mostly about a comfortably poky one-bedroom flat behind a Chinese takeaway and far too many amusing photos of cats from the internet. Now, all of a sudden, she was gorgeous, vivacious and men couldn't get enough of her. But not tonight. Tonight she just wanted a break.

What's that, girlfriend?

'You know,' she said quietly. 'Just a nice evening in. Watching some *Friends* and *Scrubs* and so on. Bottle or two of plonk, pack of ten and some Müller Rice. You know. Me time.'

Me time?

'Yeah, yesterday was quite a day, really. I dunno what to think.'

I'll tell you what to think, babe – get your arse out there and work it. There are drinks to be drunk, hunks to be had. Forget watching George Clooney – you could have George Clooney. Go out there and get him. I know I would.

'But, you know, I don't really... you know... I just fancied a bit of...'

I'll tell you a little secret, babydoll. I NEVER get bored. I don't like being bored. Being bored makes you boring. You want to know why you ended up alone? You made yourself. Get out there. Catch the eyes of a few tall, dark handsomes. You Know The Drill.

'But, I...' Emma saw her quiet night in vanishing.

That's better girl. You just listen to Cheryl. We're going to see you have a portion, all right. Tonight, my doll, we're going to paint the town red and have it large. Yeaaaaaah.

'Oh, all right then,' Emma thought to herself. 'Maybe just a quick one.'

Four hours later, Emma had sex in a car.

JACK IS PUZZLED

Cardiff didn't make sense. Jack always worried when that happened. Mysterious energy cloud, corpses, that ferry. Ianto.

He wandered down into Owen's area, and picked up one of the scans they'd done of Ianto. Everything seemed fine. Well, more than fine. He just didn't get it. He was stumped.

Then he noticed his reflection in the mirror, and blinked with surprise. He had spots.

EMMA WEBSTER IS ON A DATE

She just met him in a bar. He honestly walked up to her, all shy. This had never happened to Emma before, and she just stared at him, like a fish without anything interesting to say. Luckily, he didn't care.

'Hi, my name is Joe.' He grinned bashfully and paused. He was wearing a crumpled suit jacket, under which a striped Dennis the Menace jumper sagged. He was young and looked in need of ironing. He held out his hand, and Emma, slightly charmed, shook it. 'Look, I don't really know what to say. Hello!' he continued, looking genuinely ill-at-ease and drumming the bar.

'Pleased to meet you,' said Emma, genuinely, thinking he was quite a few steps up from the tossers at speed-dating last night. A genuine husband. She smiled. 'So, not that I'm judging you, but what do you do?'

'Oh. I edit a magazine for the National Assembly. It's OK – it's a real laugh, and my Welsh has got pretty good. Do you know any?'

'No, not really.' Emma hadn't actually sat down to learn any yet, although they had classes at lunchtime. Naturally, Vile Kate went every week.

'Actually,' continued Joe, 'I'd always been rubbish at Welsh, and felt guilty about it. I blame too much vodka at school. There was an afternoon where we all sneaked out, bought a bottle of the cheapest vodka imaginable from the only corner shop that'd sell it to us. I think it was called Perestroyka, or something. And the four of us just sat drinking at Mandy Pollard's house until Mandy threw up, and then they went back to school, and I decided that this was far more fun than learning Welsh. So I skipped all the rest of my lessons. Hadn't really needed it until now.'

Emma thought about young Joe, bunking off. He looked the kind of guy who would. Oh dear, she thought, am I starting to fancy dangerous men? She smiled at him.

'It's really handy, you know. We have to publish two versions of the magazine, but it's been really useful for the Cardiff Business Community.'

'You just pronounced that in capital letters.'

'Yes. Yes I did. Oh god. I take myself so seriously these days.' Again, his fingers drummed on the table.

'You do take yourself terribly seriously, don't you?' Emma had a sudden urge to mother him. 'What did you want to be?'

'When I grew up? A poet? Or even a writer of horror books. Ever read *The Fog?*'

'It is my favourite book!' Emma grinned, really liking him.

'Really?'

'Absolutely. I read it until the spine fell apart. No book's lived up to it apart from… Oh, I can't say.'

'I know what you're going to say.'

'You do?'

'*The Da Vinci Code.*'

'Yes! No! How did you know? I've never dared admit that to anyone.'

'I can tell. It's like KFC, Jeremy Clarkson… you know.'

'Oh, I so do.'

He is perfect.

I can tell you like him, said the voice in her head. The voice she had grown used to. The voice that had said 'chat to him, let him buy you a drink'. The voice that oozed confidence, calmness and something else. Something Emma didn't quite… like. *Relax, Emma. I'm trying to stop you from blushing. It's taking a bit of effort to calm down your body language.*

What do you mean?

Well, I'm toning down the amount of shadowing you're doing. Keeping you a bit more neutral. It gets him more interested.

Oh, ta. I dunno, though. There's something about him I like.

'Anyway, Emma – look, do you mind if I nip outside for a smoke?'

Oh damn.

Hey, Em, you smoke.

I know. But I don't want him to as well. Then I'll never give up.

But Emma, love, you don't need to – I can cure any little thing that pops up.

And him?

Yeah, I can.

But can you just stop him from smoking?

Sure.

Emma paused, wondering. What about a little bit taller?

OK. Anything else?

Oh, I could do with a cigarette, decided Emma. She was aware that Joe was looking at her. Had she zoned out? It was hard concentrating with Cheryl around sometimes. She smiled. 'Let's,' she said, reached for her packet, and slipped outside into the freezing Cardiff air.

She and Joe huddled next to each other. He grinned and handed her a light.

'Does anyone still smoke?' he asked her, cupping his hands round the cigarette.

'Just us left,' she said.

They looked at each other for a bit, and smoked quietly.

'Er, you ever thought of giving up?' asked Emma.

Joe laughed. 'Who hasn't, these days?'

She shrugged. 'I've tried a couple of times. I'm getting pretty good at it. It makes me happy.'

Joe nodded. 'Nah, I'd never give up. Unless I wanted to.'

Emma smiled. 'What if I made you?'

'Really?'

'Yeah, what if I had a machine that made you want to stop smoking, could repair all the damage, could make you… well, perfect, I guess.'

Joe laughed. 'Well, if it can repair the damage, why give up?'

'Good point,' said Emma, feeling suddenly sad. She watched Joe go back inside and sighed. 'Sorry, Joe,' she said, stubbed out her cigarette and followed him back inside.

For the second night in a row, the people of Cardiff slept badly.

JOE STERLING IS LISTED AS BEING IN A RELATIONSHIP WITH EMMA WEBSTER

Early the next morning, Joe padded out into the living room, where Emma lay stretched out over the sofa, watching TV. He kissed her on the shoulder and she turned, her gorgeous hair falling neatly out of the way.

He loved the way it did that. In fact he loved pretty much everything about her.

'Hey!' she said, in that lovely warm voice of hers.

'I missed you!' he said. 'I woke up alone in bed, and you weren't there. Is everything OK?'

'Yeah, yeah,' she said. 'I just woke up and fancied a bit of… me time. Little bit of TV and the sofa.'

'Is everything all right?' he asked, worried. 'Was I snoring? Did I take up too much of the duvet?'

She smiled, and pulled him close to her, kissing the back of his neck where his hair was neatly shaved. 'No, it's nothing,' she said softly. 'I just… it takes time for me to get used to sharing the bed with someone.'

He wrapped his arms around her. 'Well, I've got used to you already,' he breathed as he nuzzled her, and she felt the slight stubble brush across her shoulder and giggled.

'Oh, Joe,' she said. 'It's only been a few hours.'

'Yeah, I know.' Joe grinned wickedly. 'But I've never felt this way about a girl before. And I've certainly never… well, not in a car. You're wicked! And you're special.'

'Am I?'

'Yeah, you're perfect.' He kissed her again, wrapping his arms around her. 'You're perfect and you're mine.'

She sighed happily.

'I want you to meet my friends,' said Joe. 'They'll love you.'

'I'm sure they will,' sighed Emma again. She reached across for the ash tray and lit a cigarette. She offered a drag to Joe, but he shook his head. 'You know I've given up for you, babes.'

She looked at him as she dragged on her cigarette.

He sometimes wished he knew what was going on in her perfect head. He wished he could read her thoughts so that he could make her life even better. She had everything – and she wanted him. He knew he had to try very hard to live up to her. To be worthy of her.

She ran a hand through her hair. 'What's your favourite film?' she asked.

He tutted. 'You know better than to ask a bloke that. There are so many – and several of them just jostling for a place in the Top Ten. *Indiana Jones, Ghostbusters,* Proper *Star Wars,* the *Die Hards*… You know what it's like. What's yours?'

She considered. '*Breakfast At Tiffany's.*'

Joe nodded. 'Oh yeah. That's in the list. In fact it's my favourite, pretty much.'

She laughed, delighted, and kissed him. 'You're so funny!'

He looked at her, puzzled. 'No, it really is. Have I said something wrong?'

Emma's laugh died, but she continued to look at him.

He felt suddenly tired and wanted to go back to bed. 'I feel suddenly tired and want to go back to bed,' he said, and did.

Thank you.

GWEN AND IANTO GET A SHOPPING MONTAGE

Jack had insisted they go shopping.

'Just wear something natural,' Gwen had urged. Ianto had looked at her, slightly worried, and then gone off, very solemnly. Ianto emerged wearing… oh god. A tight pair of jeans, the same T-shirt as Gwen and a pretty close match for her leather jacket.

'What do you think?' he asked.

'Yeees,' said Gwen. 'You look very good. Really good. But it's not you. It's me.' Plus, if you wear that, I will have to kill you.

'But it looks so good on you,' said Ianto. Bless.

'Wear what you want. Surely you're more suits and skirts? Look around you. Really express yourself. Go crazy. And nothing orange.'

Ianto nodded, a bit panicked, and wandered off.

After three quarters of an hour they both gave up and bought him a little black dress, a sensible grey business suit and some blouses. 'I got it a size up,' explained Ianto to Gwen as they headed for the tills, 'After all, hopefully I won't be a woman for long. And then I thought you could have my clothes.'

Right, thought Gwen.

'Now,' said Ianto, smiling bravely, 'perhaps you can explain about bras.'

It was at this point that Jack called.

CAPTAIN JACK IS AVAILABLE FOR CHILDREN'S PARTIES

Jack was waiting for them in the park, holding balloons. Gwen laughed at the sight.

'Morning, girls!' he said, winking and handing them each a balloon.

Gwen took the pink one, happily. 'Jack, is there a reason for this?'

'There's always a reason, Gwen,' said Jack. 'No day is all bad if it's got balloons in it.'

Ianto looked at his, glumly. 'Mine has Mickey Mouse on it. Not a problem.'

'Cheer up,' said Jack, rubbing his balloon enthusiastically on his sleeve. 'It's time for a practical demonstration. I tell you there's a building field of static electricity around Cardiff, and what do you do?' He let go of his balloon. It started to drift up. 'You laugh.'

The balloon reached three metres above their heads. And exploded.

'Not funny any more is it?' said Jack.

'Bloody hell,' said Gwen. 'Surely that's—'

'Oh, pretty much impossible, yup,' said Jack. 'But there's an energy current flowing around Cardiff. It's been building up gently for two months. It spikes on Sunday night. Same night something strange happens to the ferry. And now little things are changing. Surge in static electricity, elevated levels of background radiation. Skeletons in bars. Ianto. Anything else?'

'Hmm,' said Gwen. 'Rhys and I have been sleeping really badly all week. Is that part of it?'

Jack nodded, excited. 'Me too! And hey, I don't sleep. Plus, I'm getting spots. And that never happens. Something's wrong with the atmosphere. So, spots, energy cloud and terrible sleep patterns. Anything else?'

Gwen let her balloon go. It floated away into the sky. 'I didn't charge it,' she said. 'Just checking.'

'Ah, an inquiring mind,' beamed Jack. 'Ianto, you want a go?'

Ianto gazed forlornly at his balloon. 'I don't want Mickey Mouse to die,' he said.

Jack patted him on the shoulder. 'It's OK,' he said. 'He doesn't have to. I just didn't want you not to have a balloon. Let's go and look at something else. It's extraordinary.'

They stood in the car park. Jack was grinning. 'Touch a car. Any car.'

Gwen picked a BMW. She'd never liked them. Jack nodded at her, approvingly. It was black, and shiny, and very new, quite expensive and – she touched it. There was the tiniest static shock. The car crumbled away.

'Oh,' said Ianto.

They looked aghast at the pile of BMW dust blowing away in the breeze.

'Quite,' said Jack. 'Just like those skeletons. Now, Tosh,' he said, tapping away at his wrist pad, as a couple of elementary maps popped up, 'Tosh would have loved this. I've managed to track the energy cloud. It built up between 2am and 3am, concentrating on this car park in Bute Park. Curious, huh?'

'CCTV?' asked Ianto.

Jack shook his head. 'The cameras are powder.'

Gwen chuckled. 'Well, there'll be witnesses. Bute car park? Dogging central! Some couple making out will have seen something happen.'

'Ah,' said Jack, shaking his head indicating several more cars marked off with Police Incident tape. 'That's why I brought you balloons. Something nice first.'

Sadly, they headed over to the cars.

EMMA WEBSTER IS WITH HER PERFECT MAN

The doorbell rang, and Emma tried not to let her heart sink. She threw open the door, and there was Joe – tall, tanned and lithe in a very expensive suit and a nice, crisp shirt. He smelled of vanilla and sandalwood, he was clean-shaven and, as he smiled, neat teeth gleaming.

She grinned, despite herself, and let him kiss her. 'You make me feel so good,' he breathed in her ear. 'I've booked us a table,' he said. 'In your favourite restaurant.'

'In our favourite restaurant,' she said, with a note of challenge.

'Of course,' he said, squeezing her tighter. 'Our favourite restaurant.'

She looked round the flat, almost desperately, until she caught a glimpse of their reflections in the mirror. They made, she had to admit, quite the perfect couple. They both looked stunning and successful, and the kind of people that others were just the tiniest bit jealous of.

She knew that when she met Joe's friends they would love her. Of course, she'd make them love her. But she liked to think that they would love her anyway.

They walked down the stairs to the taxi, Joe wrapping a protective arm around her. The taxi driver smiled at them both, proud to have such nice people in his cab. His smile was only beaten by the manager of the restaurant, so clearly happy to have them both dining that he gave them the best table, one which put them broadly on display.

Emma knew that people walking past would see such people, such a magical, loving couple, and they would think, 'Oh, I'd like to eat there.'

Joe helped her take off her coat and slid her chair in for her as she sat down. He bent over and kissed her, before sitting down and grasping her hand over the table. He sat and smiled at her.

'What are you thinking about?' she asked him.

'Nothing,' he replied and she believed him. He continued to gaze at her.

She opened the menu. He did the same.

A waitress appeared and asked what they'd like to drink.

Joe demurred. 'What would you like, Emma?'

'I don't know. Red or white. I really don't mind. You decide.'

Joe shook his head. 'No, you decide. I'm happy with what you want.'

Emma frowned, just slightly. 'A bottle of house pink, then.'

'That'll be lovely,' agreed Joe.

The waitress smiled, and went away.

They looked at the menu, Emma delighted to see that there was squid as a starter, and giant yorkshires as a main. Joe was equally happy.

'Seen anything you like?' she asked.

'Yeah. So much to choose from,' he sighed. 'I'm trying to decide between the salmon or the soup, and maybe the duck. Or a steak. I dunno.'

'Have whatever you fancy,' she assured him.

The waiter came over. Emma ordered squid and the yorkshire pudding. And Joe did the same.

When the wine came, she poured herself a large glass, and went out onto the balcony to smoke.

He got up to follow her out but she shook her head, and he stayed at the table, smiling peacefully at her, staring into the candle.

Oh my god. This is a disaster! What have I done?

You're not happy, I can tell.

Not happy? This is like hell.

What? What have I done wrong?

He's like a bloody zombie.

But haven't I done everything you wanted? I changed everything about him that you didn't like.

I know. I know. But it's like you've gone too far. Changed too much. Made him too pliant. It's not like he likes me, or loves me – he literally worships me. It's no fun.

Not even a little?

Well, it's great in bed, I'll give you that. But it's just not much fun the rest of the time. It feels wrong – like I haven't done anything to earn his love. It makes me… hate myself. He just sits there, looking at me, holding me, smiling at me, and I feel horrible. I don't deserve it. Every time he kisses me, I shrink away. I just… I don't know what to do. Is it something wrong with me, or him? Can you change the bit in me that doesn't like him?

No. That's you. I'm fairly stuck with that.

What about him?

Umph. No. That's kind of what you'll get – I've had to make some fairly drastic changes to him. If I unpick that, he'll… well, fall apart.

Oh god. Well, then maybe I'll just have to put up with it.

Not necessarily.

Really?

I can take care of him. You'll never have to see him again.

You can?

Yeah, no worries. Let's chalk this one up as a practice go. I went a bit far – I can ease back on the next one.

You're sure? And you're not cross with me?

Not a bit. This is my job, remember? I want you to be perfectly happy. And, just as we brought him into your life, so we can send him away again.

Will he be OK?

Absolutely. He'll vanish from your life like a bad dream.

And we'll find another one, someone who'll love me for me?

Of course we can. With just a couple of teensy-weensy little tweaks. But nothing big.

Promise?

Oh yeah. Don't forget – you're gorgeous. Who wouldn't want a slice of the Emma pie?

Cool. That's making me feel a whole lot better.

I can tell. But babe, you've got to keep up your side. Don't get freaked out just cos someone loves you. You're no longer a bit dumpy, a bit plain and a bit dull. You are fabulous, girl. You deserve happiness and success. You are loved because you are lovely.

To know me is to love me is to know me? Oh, Cheryl.

OK. Maybe I went a little far there. But you know what I mean. You are worth it, girlfriend, so work it. Now get back inside, you're squid's turned up. And enjoy your last meal with Joe.

Emma stubbed out her cigarette and opened the door.

She paused for a second, cold in the wind from the Bay.

'Sorry, Joe,' she said.

RHYS WILLIAMS IS COOKING UP A STORM

'Can I do anything to help?' Gwen shouted over the endless clattering of pans. A tea towel landed in her face.

'Just dry those, would you, love?' Rhys's voice came from inside the oven.

The doorbell rang, making Rhys bang his head.

'I'll go and get that,' said Gwen brightly, nipping off to get Ianto. She opened the door. Ianto stood there in the dress they'd picked out. Looking amazing.

Rhys came bounding up behind. 'Hello, Ianto, mate,' he said, his false bonhomie louder than Brian Blessed falling off Snowdon. Ianto stepped into the room, and Rhys saw him for the first time. 'Holy crap you really are a woman! And, oh, Christ, you're stunning!'

'Isn't he just?' said Gwen, laughing. 'I've not even changed yet. Showing me up, you are!'

'I wasn't complaining!' protested Rhys. 'It looks cracking on her. Doesn't it, Gwen?' Sensing the temperature plummet, he quickly added, 'Not, er, not that you don't look nice, too, love. When you make an effort.'

'Er,' said Ianto. He took another step into the room, wobbly on his heels. '… I brought a bottle.'

'Oh, that's lovely and you shouldn't have. Why don't I open

this, and you sit down, and Gwen can get changed and that?'

'Sure,' said Gwen.

She smiled at Ianto and ran off to the bedroom, thinking 'This is a terrible, terrible mistake.'

Rhys poured the wine out into two glasses, and then quickly stirred the saucepans.

'So, ah, you're a woman now, then?'

'Yes.'

'Been one long?'

'No. Just this week.'

'Oh. Is it permanent?'

'I don't know.'

'Well, it's a change, I suppose.'

'Yes, I suppose it is.'

'Does it feel much different?'

'Yes. A bit.'

'I suppose it would. But you're OK?'

'As far as I can tell.'

'Good. Good. I, ah, made risotto.'

'Nice.'

'You do still eat risotto, don't you?'

'Why wouldn't I?'

'No, sorry. You're right. I just meant now that you're, er—'

'Rhys, I'm a woman, not an alien.'

'No, no, of course not. And a very lovely woman at that.'

'Um. Thank you.'

'I mean, mate, no offence, but I've been dying to say – you've got a smashing pair of – ah, Gwen, love, wine?'

'Yes please.' Gwen entered the room, her voice as crisp as lettuce. 'Oh, you got Pinot Grigio! How lovely.'

Gwen poured as much wine as the glass would take, and settled down to look at Ianto, who glanced away immediately, embarrassed. He mouthed 'sorry' to her, and she smiled back, tightly. Behind them, all Gwen could hear was Rhys loudly stirring a saucepan.

'Nice flat,' said Ianto, after a while.

'You've been here before,' said Gwen, more icily than she intended, but Ianto didn't seem abashed.

'I know, but normally in a crisis. You know – alien baby, dead body, or temporal paradox. Never really had a chance to take in the décor. It's very nice.'

'Thank you, mate!' bellowed Rhys. 'I did most of the work, you know. And the cleaning.'

'It's true,' said Gwen, as Rhys started to spoon out food onto plates. 'I'm all over the place with housework – but I blame it on the hours.'

'And truth to tell,' said Rhys, bringing over the plates, 'it's no hardship.' He put Ianto's food down in front of him. 'But there's no doubting who wears the trousers in this marriage.'

Gwen lashed out with her foot, but just missed Rhys's shin. Ianto gazed emptily at his risotto.

'Lovely,' he said, quietly. 'Thank you for going to so much trouble.'

'Don't mention it,' said Rhys, settling down. 'It's a pleasure. We're here for you. Really, mate. It must be a tough time for you.'

Gwen picked at her food. 'What does that mean? It's not so bad being a girl, you know.'

Rhys was starting to wear the stricken look of a hunted animal. 'No. Ah. No, of course not. I just meant that it must be a shock. A bit of a change. You know – when you've got used to… well. You know.' He then began a really ill-advised mime.

'Bits,' said Ianto quietly. Gwen dropped her fork.

Rhys carried on digging. 'Yes. Tackle. An inside leg.'

'My father was a tailor,' said Ianto.

'Really? What does he think of your, ah, new outfit, eh?' asked Rhys, helplessly.

'I haven't spoken to him,' said Ianto. 'He's dead, really.' He smiled a little.

Two hours later, Gwen closed the door with relief and sank down against it. Rhys came up behind her and wrapped his arms round her. She could feel him shaking with laughter.

She turned round and kissed him.

'You're in such deep, deep trouble, Mr Williams,' she said.

'Was that not the worst dinner party of all time?' he asked.

'Probably. We are never cooking for any of my work colleagues ever again.'

'But you have to admit, my risotto was pretty bloody spectacular.'

'It was. Oh, Rhys, never change.'

'There's precious little danger of that.'

JOE STERLING IS DUMPED

Out in Penarth is an old Victorian pier that stretches out into the Bay. In summer it's crowded with ice cream and hot dogs and fishermen and laughing children thundering up and down the old planks. But in winter it is a desolate iron ghost. Especially at night, creaking and cracking like a wrecked galleon.

No one was on the pier that night. The rain was too heavy even for walking the dog. So, no one passed by the last little shelter on the pier. No one noticed the figure in the natty suit sat on the bench, staring out to sea, a sad expression on his still face, the tracks of tears frozen on his cheeks.

The figure didn't move, didn't feel the cold, didn't feel the rain which coiled up and down the pier.

Gradually, the fine suit became wetter and wetter, soaked through to the skin, the bone and the bench beneath. And, as the storm poured on, the figure just washed away, a sodden ash that spread out across the boards, trickling down through the cracks and into the sea.

Emma Webster is no longer listed as being in a relationship

SERGEANT PEPPER IS A LONELY HEART'S CLUB BAND

Jack swept into the Hub's boardroom, eyes shining. 'Ladies! Tonight we're going speed-dating!'

Ianto will bloody love this, thought Gwen. She looked across at him, all shining in his smart little woman's business suit, the skirt stopping well above the knee. 'Marvellous!' she mouthed, while at the same time thinking, 'Bit trampy, Ianto.'

Jack coughed. 'As I was saying. Tonight, according to Patrick Matthew's Facebook group, his speed-dating group meets. Little Miss Death may well be there. Tonight might even be the night she meets him. So we should be there too.'

Gwen snorted. 'Come off it, Jack. Have you seen the kind of people who go on these things?' She pointed towards the list of people who 'may be attending'. 'They're not exactly conventionally attractive are they? I mean, there's a few I wouldn't kick out of bed, but you know, they all look a bit… normal.'

Jack leaned over. 'What are you saying, *Mrs Williams*?'

'Well, I hate to admit it…' Gwen really hated to admit it. 'But you and Ianto aren't exactly speed-dating material. Ianto's drop dead gorgeous, and you're—'

'Too good to be true?' Jack smiled broadly. 'It's the twinkle in my eye.'

'Not exactly, no,' said Gwen, carefully. 'I just don't think you'd do your best work.'

'Are you kidding? I'd be brilliant.'

'I'm sure you would, Jack,' said Gwen patiently. 'But I don't think we'd learn anything. You'd just walk out of there with a pile of phone numbers, some broken hearts and a hickey.'

'That would be from Ianto,' sighed Jack. 'Too much of the teeth.'

Gwen gently stirred her coffee and idly wondered how often the two of them actually had sex. She suspected that most of the time they just stood in a room naked, hands on hips, pouting at each other.

Ianto just looked deeply embarrassed. 'I think Gwen's right.'

'Great,' said Gwen. 'I'll pop home and change.'

EMMA WEBSTER IS SELECTING HER NEXT VICTIM

Hi, I'm Martin. My friends call me Marty.
OK. Now, I'm gonna pass based purely on the dress sense.

Hello. Hi. I'm Selwyn. I've never done this before. I'm with the
Hmm. Can we give him better – is it teeth? Or hair? I dunno.

Hi, I'm William. My friends call me Bill, and I hope you will too.
We can't fix tosser, can we?

Hi, I'm Harry. I'm
Oh. He looks amazing. Can we make him just a little taller?

Greetings!
No.

Hi, I'm Rhys. I work in haulage.
Yes!

GWEN IS LOSING THE ARGUMENT

Gwen let herself very quietly into the flat. It was a move she'd practised from back in the days when she still went out, taking her shoes off on the stairs and sneaking in giggling, trying not to wake up Rhys, who'd almost always be sat on the sofa, waiting up for her, passed out among a jungle of pizza and beer bottles. Once she'd even found him and Banana Boat, stretched out, game controls in their hands, as riderless cars zoomed round and round on the screen. How long ago was that? It had been ages. Honestly, you turn thirty, you get married, you vow the party won't stop, but—

'Love?' Rhys was wandering through from the bedroom. Gwen froze, caught quivering on the step. She switched on her best smile. 'Hiiiiiii…' she managed. It never failed.

'Right,' said Rhys, folding his arms.

Damn.

'What're you doing home? I thought you were working tonight.'

'I am,' Gwen tried stretching the smile a tiny little bit further, but Rhys just walked closer.

'You are up to something.'

'Uh-huh,' said Gwen, pottering through to the kitchen. He followed her. Bad sign. She turned. 'Look, it's undercover work.

Nothing dangerous, but I'm just popping in for a change of clothes. You know. Don't want to stick out.'

Rhys's gaze continued to stare, pitiless and unblinking, at her jeans, T-shirt and leather jacket. It was at times like this he reminded her of her dad – Gwen could wrap him round her finger, unless he wheeled out the hard stare. Gwen sometimes wondered if Dad had taught it to Rhys.

She took a couple of steps towards the fridge, took out a can, opened it, and started to drink. All the while Rhys stared on.

'Oh,' she said, toughing it out, brightly, 'I don't suppose the immersion's on is it? I've just got time for a shower, and then I can be all out of your way.'

Rhys tilted his head to one side and smiled. It was a dangerous smile. 'Normally, if it's Torchwood, an evening out involves you running through muddy tunnels. Suddenly you're coming home for new clothes and a shower. Now, I don't believe Jack's got classier, has he, love?'

'Well, no,' Gwen admitted. 'Look – I just don't want you worrying.'

'I worry every time you go to work in the morning.' Rhys's voice was rising a little. 'I worry every time I try and call you and I can't get through. I worry about you, full stop.'

Aww, bless, thought Gwen, and nearly kissed him. 'Look, it's really easy, Rhys. Something's killing people. Remember the corpse I found at the restaurant? It's not the only one. Several men have died on dates in the last week. So… I'm going speed-dating.' She finished, quickly and bravely.

Rhys moved smoothly towards the kettle and pulled down two mugs before she could blink.

'Speed-dating, is it?' he said. 'Not even married a few months,' he sighed, stirring the tea bags and pouring in milk. With a practised move, the bags were flipped into the bin and the mugs carried smoothly across the living room towards the coffee table.

Oh god, thought Gwen, we're going to have a rational conversation. Sometimes, I miss the rows.

A few minutes later, they were having a very good-sized row. Gwen was shouting. 'No! Rhys! No! I am not having you come along!'

Rhys roared back. 'What, are you frightened I might get more attention than you?'

'No, of course not!'

'Thanks very much, pet.'

'No! You know what I mean – this isn't fair. I can't spend the evening worrying about you.'

'Then don't. I've been on dates with mental girls before. I've even married one, and it's going bloody well, thank you very much.'

Gwen marvelled at how determined Rhys's jaw had got. She suddenly saw a glimpse of him as a child really, really wanting a toy fire engine. She spoke, gently. 'I see. And how will you know if it's the suspect you're talking to?'

'Well, I'm assuming two things will happen. One, she'll try and kill me, two, you'll come down on her like a ton of bricks.'

'Ten points to Gryffindor,' said Gwen.

'Admit it – you're looking for a woman. You going along is a bit pointless. What'll you be looking for?'

'I don't know – desperation, anxiety, hunger.'

'I see. You've not been out with single women for a while, have you? Good luck spotting the difference there, pet.'

'Rhys – how many single women do you have throwing themselves at you?'

Rhys shrugged. 'Company Christmas Do, they hurl themselves at me like Blu-Tack.'

Gwen couldn't help but laugh. 'Bollocks.'

Rhys placed a placating hand on her arm. 'Now don't fret, love. I may possess a raw animal magnetism, but I swear I've only ever used my powers for good.'

'Really?'

'Yeah. I know what single women are looking for – someone dependable, reliable, and studly.'

'But what about the single men?'

Rhys smiled wolfishly. 'Something blonde, fit, and easier to get into than a tangerine.'

HELENA CARTER IS MAKING MONEY FROM THE MISERY OF OTHERS

The manager of Abalone's shot Gwen a worried look when she walked in. She ignored it, and headed over to a girl at a table with a lot of stickers.

'Hi!' she said.

The girl looked up, and grinned, professionally.

Gwen eyed her up and didn't like her. The woman was very polished. Everything about her reminded Gwen of the people who came in to do training courses when she was in the police. Great, great people skills but as shallow as a bucket. All open questions and big smiles and no bloody use in a crisis.

'Hello! Welcome! Is this your first time at speed-dating?'

'Er, yes. Yes it is.'

'Lovely,' said the woman. 'Well, it's ten pounds, it'll be a lovely evening, and there's a free cocktail at the bar. What's your name?'

'Gwen Cooper.'

The woman looked at Gwen for a beat, and then wrote out 'Gwen Cooper', and handed it to her on a sticky badge.

Gwen grinned goofily. 'Why do they never make these things nice so that they don't ruin an outfit, eh?'

The woman looked at the badge. 'Please don't take it off. We've got some gorgeous men here tonight and we'll be kicking off in a couple of minutes. Why not have a mingle and enjoy your complimentary Bellini?'

Gwen swished to the bar, where a small group of women were nervously making scrabbling small talk. In a corner, like they were penned up, a clutch of men stood. They looked sullen.

'Oh god,' Gwen thought. 'None of these people look like killers. This is just going to be a completely embarrassing nightmare.'

And then Rhys walked in.

Gwen picked up her free cocktail, downed it, and walked swiftly to the loo.

Rhys walked in, in time to see Gwen darting to the loo. He grinned and marched up to the table.

'Evening, luv. I'm here to find the love of my life, or whatever comes along.' He smiled and the woman gave him a plastic flicker of interest.

'Well, it's ten pounds, it'll be a lovely evening, and there's a free cocktail at the bar. What's your name?'

As Rhys told her she scribbled on a sticker and continued in a flat voice, 'Please go and join the bachelors. Don't forget the lovely free cocktail or beer waiting for you at the bar. We'll be starting in just a few minutes.' She put the sticker on him.

'Hey!' said Rhys. 'You'd think they'd come up with something that didn't ruin an outfit.'

He walked off, and the woman at the desk watched him go, curious.

'We're going to be late,' said Emma.

Yes, but you look fabulous. You have nothing to worry about.

'Really?'

Of course. If there was anything wrong with you, you know I would fix it. I'm not letting you in there unless you're perfect, girlfriend.

'Perfect?' Emma liked the word and repeated it.

Yes. You're going to be the best person there. You know it. You can have whoever you want. Now go on – let's make a storm.

Emma pushed open the door.

As she walked in, she breathed in, closed her eyes, and then opened them. First she took in the group of women at the bar, all of them turning to look at her. Emma gave them all a wide, unthreatening smile. She could hear Cheryl's voice in her head: *You are better than them!* But she didn't, she couldn't believe it. Some of the women smiled back. It was the kind of look of quiet comradeship and sympathy that women gave each other when stuck waiting for an unfairly late bus.

She looked at the men in their little area. She noticed some quiet nudging and glancing in her direction. Hello, boys, she thought, and gave them the curiously bored look that Cheryl had taught her.

She barely glanced down at the woman running the speed-dating. 'Emma Webster,' she said, taking the sticker and placing it proudly on her lapel before striding to the bar.

Helena Carter had been running speed-dating for a few years. It made her a tidy little profit. She did, it was true, work in PR. But she found this a nice little sideline, and, as she told her few friends, 'I really feel nice – it's making a difference in people's lives, that's what it is, you know. I'm really giving something back.'

If you'd asked for her opinion of Gwen, Rhys and Emma, it would have gone as follows.

Gwen: Don't go giving yourself airs that you're too good for this, darling. You're not. You're here, aren't you? You'll be lucky to find something with an attitude like that. And I think you bite your nails. I've seen your type. Three speed-dates in, and you start slugging back the cocktails, and then you're either being helped into a taxi, or a man called Barry.

Rhys: Aw, what a sweetheart. He'll do very well here. First-timer. I can tell – a bit nervous, but a real sweetie. Bet you he has a lovely flat and a nice job. Good old bit of Welsh charm – and there's nothing wrong with that. If he doesn't get snapped up, I'll try and see if he needs a bit of coaching. I bet he's not been back on the scene for long. Perhaps he's just out of a marriage. Oh. I could take those broken wings and make you fly.

Emma: What is she doing back here? I mean, it's unsettling. She looks so good – has she been dieting, or sprayed on the tan, or just found a new hairdresser? I dunno, but she looks knockout, the cow. Of course, I shouldn't begrudge her her looks, but she's really come on in leaps and bounds. She's made an effort. She used to look like she'd been dressed by her cat. Ah well. If there's hope for her, there's hope for all of us.

Emma got herself a drink from the bar, and inhaled it, glancing around nervously.

Bloody chill, girlfriend! Leave everything to me, and you know you'll be brilliant.

Yeah, thought Emma. I'll just look at a few people, and if I don't like them, then I can go home, we'll log in to *Are You Interested?* and laugh at strange men's curtains.

God, you are thrilling. And I'm taking the liberty of tweaking your metabolism just a little. A little less adrenalin, a little more…

Ahhhhhhhhhhhhhhhhhhhh. Emma decided this was the best drink she'd ever tasted. She caught her reflection in the mirror and grinned. I am looking fantastic, aren't I?

See? Now, let's get on with this.

'Hello, my name is Harry. I work in… well, it's just a call centre really. At the moment. It's not what I wanted to do, really, but you know how it is – you doss around after uni, and then you do something for a few weeks, then a few weeks more, and before you know it, you've been doing it for eighteen months, and then you're the manager. But you know, it's OK – the people are great, and the money's nice, but my real love is my sport and my mates and surfing. Do you know what the original lyrics to that Beach Boys song were?'

Emma sipped carefully at her drink.

Well?

He is gorgeous, she admitted. He's got great hair, lovely teeth and piercing blue eyes. And I can tell he's ripped. She let herself imagine them taking walks along a foreign beach. They looked good together.

But…?

Well, he's so dull. I can just tell. And so young.

What do you want me to change?

I dunno.

Oh, Emma!

Look, the body's perfect, but he's so empty. I mean, can you make him more mature, teach him a foreign language, get him a decent job, some nicer jeans and a cordon bleu cookery course?

…

What was that?

Emma love, there's nothing I wouldn't do for you, doll. You know that. But there are limits. Yeah, I can give him more balls, and make him a bit brighter. I can also have a bit of a fiddle with the genes that predispose him to cheating.

Cheating?

Oh yes. I'm afraid he's never been faithful in a relationship. Those cheekbones were built for cheating. He gave his last girlfriend the clap. And her best friend got it too. And while he's here making puppy eyes at you, there's a girl in Newport who thinks he's The One. But I can change all that. I can make him faithful and pox free.

I don't know. Would he be the same?

Look, I am bending over backwards for you, sweet cheeks. You've got the best-looking fella in the room, and he's desperate for you. Look, if he's not a keeper, we can at least get you a shag out of him.

Oh, cheers, Cheryl.
Someone has got very choosy of late.
Of course! I'm nearly perfect, aren't I?
:-)

Gwen watched as the guy sat down. Ponytail, (too) skinny jeans, black T-shirt with a skull design made 3-D by his beer belly. Too much jewellery. And, oh yes, a mobile phone in a holster. He gave her a big grin, and she just thought, 'Spots? In your thirties? Oh bless.'

'Gavin,' he said, and laughed nervously. 'This is all right, isn't it?'

'Yeah,' said Gwen. 'I suppose. I'm Gwen.'

'Pleased to meet you,' he said. 'So, are you into modelling?'

Gwen giggled, despite herself. 'Bless you! No! God, no! When I was twenty and a twiglet, maybe. But no, not now!'

'Shame,' the man sighed, genuinely disappointed. 'I paint orcs myself.'

'What?'

'Model orcs.'

'Right. Uh.' Gwen fingered her glass. How do people do this? 'Any other hobbies?'

'I love going to the cinema. And gaming. MonstaQuest. And do you play Warcraft?'

'Dear god, no! My friend Owen used to, all the time.'

'Really? What's his username?'

'Oh, he doesn't play much any more,' admitted Gwen, tightly.

'Pity. I hate it when someone leaves their Guild,' the man looked genuinely sad. 'Still, I bet I've whipped him a few times.'

'Are you sure? I think he was pretty good.'

Gavin managed a surprisingly roguish grin. 'I think I'm better.'

'OK.' Gwen thought hard and mustered an interest. What was

it the Gavins of the world loved? She tried to remember what the staff were talking about whenever she went to dig Rhys out of Spillers Records. 'So, what about the cinema – I'm guessing films with a high body count and a big space bang at the end?'

He shrugged. 'Actually, I'm more into my visceral horror – you know, torture porn? Love that stuff!'

'Really? I've always been a bit squeamish, me,' said Gwen. 'Never could stand the sight of blood.' She looked long and hard at Gavin. Do I really have to talk to this moron for a whole five minutes?

'Shame,' continued Gavin. 'There used to be a few clubs in Cardiff, you know...' He leaned forward, conspiratorially, his breath catching Gwen like a force field. 'Tales of all sorts of horrors. Like fight club – but with beasts.'

'What kind of beasts?' Gwen was genuinely intrigued.

'Well, you see, people said it was aliens. Aliens fighting humans. But I don't believe all that. There's a lot of conspiracy theories – you know how it is with all the stuff that's been going on in the last couple of years.'

'Yeah,' said Gwen, almost impossibly slowly.

'But lots of it's nuts. I mean – all this talk of alien visits, and ships in the sky and so on. But it's all "a friend of a friend", isn't it? Have you ever met anyone who's actually met an alien? Talked to one? No? I thought not.' Gavin smiled in a satisfied way.

'No. Not me. I've always lived a quiet life,' said Gwen.

'Oh, don't get me wrong – it's not all blood and gore for Mr Gavin. Sometimes, I like nothing better than to chill at home with a pizza and some boxsets. That can be dead romantic, can't it?'

'Oh god, can it?' sighed Gwen.

One thing that should have alerted Gwen to the nearby presence of an alien device is the fact that this conversation had only taken ten seconds. She had another four minutes and fifty seconds of speed-dating with Gavin to go. And nothing more to say to him.

Emma was talking to some poor kid. He was babbling away about how awful his flat was. 'See, this bloke moved back to help his folks run a cinema. He let it out dead cheap, and I thought I had a bargain. Real impressive it is – at the back of an old warehouse. The square footage is amazing, although the bathroom leaks.'

Emma was nodding quietly, trying to imagine him with better skin, or a clean T-shirt, maybe, or a bit Scottish, or blond or something.

'Thing is, it really is an old warehouse. If I meet a girl out and she comes home, she thinks I'm like a serial killer or something. Honestly, before I even start unbolting the hangar door they're phoning a cab...'

'And, actually, at the moment, I'm really into World Music.'

PATRICK MATTHEWS IS VERY MUCH STILL ALIVE

Patrick lifted the rubbish out onto the dumpster. He spun when he heard the footsteps behind him.

'God!' he breathed. 'Ianto! You nearly scared me to death.'

The girl looked genuinely alarmed. 'Really? Oh, I hope not. I really hope not. Sorry. Didn't mean to startle you.'

Patrick smiled. 'You didn't, eh? Then what you doing creeping up on me in a dark alley?'

Ianto looked bemused. 'I'm surprisingly used to alleys.'

'Is that so?' He smiled again, and leaned closer. 'So you really checking up on me, or just trying for a quick snog without Bren noticing?'

Up close, Patrick smelt of fresh hot oil and vinegar. Ianto realised he was breathing quickly. 'Er,' he said.

'Yes?' Patrick smiled, really amused.

'Everything been all right? In the shop, and all?' Oh god, I'm babbling, thought Ianto.

'Yes. Fine. Couple of boys decided to kick off tonight, but I soon cleared them out. I'm so glad I played a lot of rugby at school.'

'Yeah, always comes in handy,' said Ianto. 'Um. Girl's rugby. Obviously.'

'Obviously, yeah,' Patrick smirked, and started to undo his

apron strings. 'So, is that it?'

Ianto nodded, eagerly. 'Honestly, genuinely, just checking up on you. You're alive, tick, good. Carry on.'

'And?' Patrick leaned back against the wall, smirking.

Ianto looked round, and slumped with defeat. 'Oh all right, but just a quick snog.'

GWEN HAS HAD BETTER NIGHTS

Gwen sat down and scowled at the man opposite her.

'Hello, I'm Gwen,' she said flatly.

'Hello, ugly, I'm Rhys,' the man said back to her. He was grinning like a smug cat.

'And what do you do for a living?'

'Aw, I break hearts, I do, darling. How about you?'

Gwen shrugged. 'I work for a top-secret organisation that protects Cardiff from alien invasion. I like to think I'm bloody good at it. What about you? Moved any vans around in a timely fashion recently?'

Rhys grinned broadly. 'Oh, a few. So. Single are you?'

'Oh yes,' nodded Gwen. 'Well, more widowed, really.'

'Is that so? Tragic.' Rhys tutted. 'What killed him? Was it your cooking?'

'Noooo,' Gwen assured him, brightly. 'One day, he spent so much time on the sofa that it ate him.' She swilled down the dregs of the third complimentary Bellini she'd managed to grab from the bar. She was getting a bit giggly. Probably from all the small talk.

'You know,' said Rhys, smiling back at her, 'you remind me of my last girlfriend. Only she had less split ends, you know.'

'When this is over...'

'We're getting chips?'

Gwen shrugged. 'Maybe, maybe not. I'm being unpredictable. I've heard it adds spice to a relationship. Now – seen any psychos?'

Rhys shook his head. 'Apart from my wife, no. Everyone's been very sweet, actually. You?'

Gwen shook her head. 'Let's just say I've discovered I could do worse.'

'That's charming, that is,' said Rhys.

'Do you want chips on the way home or not?'

Helena tinkled a little bell, signalling time to change partners. 'Aw, and I was having such a laugh,' Rhys stood up. 'So do you want to see me again?'

'Not as long as I live,' said Gwen.

Rhys left Gwen, grinning. It hadn't, to be truthful, been a great night for the Williams ego. Not that he'd let Gwen know. No, as far as she was concerned, it had been all honey and roses. But it had also been a nasty reminder of what the world outside his little nest was like.

True, there were times when all he remembered was the fun of being single, that mad prehistoric time before he met Gwen. Those rare golden nights when it was way past booze o'clock, somewhere in between kebab and the last pint sinking like lead… that lovely, carefree moment when a girl would look at you across the Walkabout and her eyes would stay on you for a bit long, and Lottery Clive would nudge you on the shoulder and say 'Wahey – you're in there.' And you'd pretend not to notice, but you'd look back, and she'd look back, and then…

Oh, the fun of it all.

As far as he could remember.

Compared to all those evenings in, waiting for Gwen not to turn up. Feeling a bit like his mum, waiting up for his dad to get back from a late shift, and trying not to flinch when he breathed beer over her while she laid out the tea things and straightened down the tablecloth.

Or those cold evenings alone in the flat, when Daveo was out, and Banana Boat was off on one of his Grail quests, and it was just Rhys and the TV guide, suddenly it all felt a bit wrong. So empty. So lonely. And then, eventually, normally a bottle of beer too late, the key would turn in the lock, and there would be Gwen, all big smiles and hurried apologies and bright, bright enthusiasm for whatever he could salvage from the risotto. And it would be like they were on stage, in a play. The Gwen and Rhys Show. Was it a comedy, or a tragedy?

And they'd lie in bed together later, and he'd notice that she no longer clung to him while she slept, and he'd kiss her sleeping shoulder gently and he'd think, 'Is this as good as it's ever going to get?'

And, now, here he was, discovering that for all those quiet nights in and all those times when they talked at each other – what they had was better. What they had was so much better.

Rhys stared down at the table for just a second before looking into the eyes of Date #12. He didn't want to see the expression. He just didn't. He'd seen four different versions of naked, fearful desperation. He'd heard six different nervous, self-deprecating laughs. One girl whose first word had been sorry. Then a woman who'd not even blinked, but just spoken in a dull, weary tone – not just bored, but despairing – both of Rhys and herself – without hope. And three women who gave it the full 'tude – all Valley pouts and aye-aye body language and bosoms which heaved above their dresses like whales on an ice floe.

After a tide of all it – all of that like me, hate me, ignore me but please want me, Rhys just felt psychologically battered. No one, not even Gwen, would have rushed to describe Rhys as sensitive, but if asked to point out the serial killer among the women, his response would have been 'narrow it down, love.'

Frankly, though, what he'd seen of the men had dispirited

him. There were a few nice, normal blokes. Bit on the sweaty side, mind, but tidy enough. A couple of nice chaps who were a bit pie-friendly, sure, and one guy who looked lost away from his computer (ponytail and a mobile phone on a hip holster. Nice). And then, frankly, it all got a bit oh dear. Rhys gazed into the bottom of the barrel, and the bottom of the barrel gazed back at him. Nylon shirts, Simpsons ties, comb-overs, dandruff and Simon Cowell trousers. It was all here and it was all mad. No wonder someone out there was wiping out the single men of Cardiff. They were probably mercy killings.

And so, with that peace made, Rhys stepped forward and sat down.

'Oh. Hi, I'm Rhys,' he said, trying not to boggle.

'And I'm Emma,' said the woman of his dreams.

Rhys didn't know what to say next, but she leant over. He could smell her perfume, which was subtle and expensive. He loved how she was dressed – classy dress without being showy, sexy without being revealing. Great hair, a lovely smile, and just the sense that she'd stepped off a movie set. That smile – and the laugh in her eyes. It put him at ease, made him want her to like him.

'Don't worry,' she said, like she was letting him in on the joke. 'No one knows what to say at these things.'

He shrugged. '"Hi, I'm Rhys. I work in haulage." That usually about does it for me,' Rhys admitted.

Oddly, she didn't seem to be listening for a moment – but then her eyes lit up. 'Excuse me,' she said. 'I got distracted by the music they play in here. I swear it's the *Top Gun* soundtrack.'

Rhys paused, impressed. 'Good call. You're right.'

'Musical genius, me,' she admitted. 'I can name that crap in three notes or less.'

'That's quite a skill,'

'Yeah – utterly useless, but it impresses the boys.'

'It certainly does.' Rhys suddenly, genuinely liked her. She seemed relaxed about the whole thing. She was dating and flirting and didn't remind him at all of a slightly dusty Garfield clinging to a rear windscreen.

'So what's on your iPod?' she asked.

'Oh, that's not fair.' Rhys was stumped. 'You know I'm going to try and give you a cool answer.'

She shook her head. 'Absolutely not. I want to know what you listened to when you came here through the rain. I bet you nodded your head.'

'Actually, er…' Oh, I'd make such a bad spy. 'Well, I walked.'

'And didn't listen to any music?'

'Yes, well, er, that is…' Now Rhys, don't start this with a lie. 'Well, actually, I walked down with someone.'

'Someone?' Emma, amused, held up her hands and made quote marks.

'My ex, Gwen. She's not very happy about me moving on.'

She stroked his hand, just slightly, and Rhys suddenly felt like he'd discovered a new flavour of ice cream. 'I'm sorry about that, Rhys,' she said.

'Oh, it's not so bad, really. She just can't accept that it's over. I'm trying to be gentle, but we weren't working. It was her job – she saw more of it than she did me, and one day I just got tired of waiting for her to come home.'

'I'm sorry to hear that,' she said. 'Work's just work, isn't it?'

'Yeah,' said Rhys, warming to the subject, 'but she didn't get that – not until I'd moved out. And now she wants me back. But I am saying no.'

'Good for you.' Again, a light touch, just a little bit higher up his arm.

'Thing is, she says she'll change. Says she'll be different, you know, just to please me. And that's not what I want. I'm just me. And work is part of what she is. She shouldn't try and be what she's not just to make me happy. I never will.'

The bell rang. Rhys's face crumpled. 'Oh, I'm sorry.'

And Emma laughed. 'Rhys, love. Just a tip – next time, say Simon and Garfunkel.'

'What?'

'If you're asked what you were listening to just say Simon and Garfunkel. They're safe, make you seem sensitive, and if you're challenged you can shrug and say it was on shuffle and that you've got tickets to the Ting Tings next month. But whatever you do, don't talk about your ex!'

Rhys spread out his hands, aghast. 'I am so, so sorry… That is so tragic.'

Emma shook her head. 'It's OK. You'll know for next time.' And she smiled with all her teeth.

Next time? Rhys walked away, just a little bit of a spring in his step.

'You were bloody all over her,' spat Gwen as they stormed down Chippie Alley.

'Was not.' Rhys tried lingering meaningfully outside his favourite kebabery, but Gwen was having none of it and didn't even break her stride.

'You practically licked the air she breathed.'

'She was well put-together, I'll give her that.'

'You could have been a bit more subtle. I thought you were supposed to be playing it cool?'

'Heart on my sleeve, me. Always been my trouble. Salt of the earth.'

'Well, she's instantly suspect number one.'

'You're jealous! Just cos something wonderful steps into my world, you want to taser her and stick her in a cell next to a Weevil.'

'Next to? She can bloody share a cell.'

'Gwen, love?'

'Yes.'

'You're bloody magnificent when you're jealous.'

'Thank you. Is there any of that lasagne left in the fridge?'

'A little.'

'Then you are my perfect man.'

'I still bet I get more calls than you do.'

EMMA WEBSTER IS A MARKED WOMAN

Gwen waited until Rhys was asleep, and then slipped out of bed and drove to the Hub. She loved the furtive feeling of wandering across the empty plaza, stepping up to the fountain, and then the click and the cold rush of night air as the invisible lift carried her down.

Sensing her presence, lights flickered gently into action, lighting up each of the storeys that the lift carried her through. Little pathways across the Hub's floor lit up, and she stepped over to her desk, switched her computer on, then went over to put the kettle on. Ianto wasn't around, so she figured she could make a cup of instant without getting into trouble. She guiltily kept a tiny jar hidden in her workstation. She'd tried telling him once that instant wasn't so bad, really, but he'd just stared at her, like she was giving the 'Rivers of Blood' speech.

Once into the system, she uploaded the digital pictures she'd taken of the room, along with details of the people on the register. She watched as the complicated alien machinery at the heart of Torchwood's computer reached out into the internet, cross-matching faces and names and pulling in information – phone numbers, more photos, blog posts, one small criminal record, a wish list from Amazon, a history of dodgy dealings on eBay, some ill-advised beach photos from Facebook, a video of a restored car from YouTube, and proof that Gavin was quite the best player of Warcraft in Cardiff. But there was one name and face that Gwen homed in on. She clicked her mouse, and watched as Emma Webster floated forward, gradually filling the screen. Another click, a slight fumble, a small curse, two right clicks, and more images of her from over the years popped up on several other monitors that flickered into life.

'She is gorgeous.'

Gwen screamed and jumped.

Bugger.

There, holding out a cup of freshly brewed coffee, was Ianto. He looked a million dollars in a neat little dress with kicky heels, like he'd been to a board meeting, followed swiftly by a cocktail party and an awards ceremony.

Gwen sat there, guilty and dishevelled, in the old sweatpants she sometimes slept in and a baggy T-shirt, her hand still clasped in shock to her breast, waiting for her breath to come back.

'Ianto! Don't do that!' She was furious with herself for being scared.

'I'm so sorry. I thought you'd like some coffee. I really didn't mean to scare you.'

'And what are you doing looking like Grace Kelly?'

Ianto looked a bit blank. 'Like what?' He glanced down. 'Oh this? Oh, it's nothing, really. Just something I found in the Archive. Turns out there's tonnes down there. Sometimes it's nice to wear really good clothes. I've always felt comfortable in smart clothes – you know how it is, stick with what makes you feel comfy.' He glanced at Gwen, and smiled.

Gwen felt herself curling up. Especially when she realised there were still bits of lasagne stuck to her T-shirt.

'Yeah,' she said slowly.

Ianto stepped forward and settled the cup down. 'Truthfully, I didn't feel much like going to sleep. I've not been sleeping well. Nothing really planned. Did a bit of tidying in the vaults.'

'No Jack?'

Ianto shrugged. 'Still out trying to track down the cause of his static cloud. You know how he is. So what's all this, then?'

Reluctantly, Gwen turned her attention back to the screen. 'Well, Rhys and I went to that speed-dating thing.'

Ianto smiled. 'Taking your husband speed-dating is so modern.'

'Yeah. He turned out to be quite useful, actually. More useful than Jack would have been.'

'I'm always useful!' Jack strode in from nowhere, flinging his coat onto the sofa. He adopted his big beam. 'Twenty strangers, some alcohol, and a chance to make small talk? Thirty minutes and we'd all have been in a big naked heap.'

'Exactly,' said Gwen. 'Lovely fun for you, I'm sure, Jack, but we wouldn't have learnt anything. Whereas Rhys and I—'

'I think it's sweet,' put in Ianto.

'We learned a lot. I think. I had a hunch about one of the women there. It turns out she's one of the women missing from Tombola's. And that's not all.'

Jack looked at the screens, filled with pictures of Emma Webster. 'Her?'

'Yes.'

'Quite the babe. I would. I definitely would. Wouldn't you, Ianto?'

'If you promised not to film it, Jack, then yes.'

My eyes, thought Gwen. 'Anyway – Emma Webster. Here's the youngest picture we've got.' A school photo flashed up. It showed Emma in her late teens, a bit sullen, a bit spotty, still a bit of puppyfat. Surrounded by her classmates, she just looked cold and unhappy.

Jack leaned in closely, smiling fondly. 'You know, I'm in one of my school photos three times. The Time Agency gave me a medal and a small fine.'

Gwen pressed on. 'Look – here she is at her thirtieth birthday party. A couple of weeks ago.'

'Yeah. Better. She's grown up well.'

'Yeah – but… she's not… jaw-dropping. She either's really made an effort for speed-dating, or something… different's going on here. I mean look – here she is last night.'

They looked. They saw what she meant.

'It's not like she's had work done, it's just like she's… better.'

'Emma 2.0,' said Ianto.

Jack nodded. 'Now she's… stunning. She's perfect.'

Perfect. They both looked at Ianto.

He coughed. 'I'll go and make some more coffee, shall I?'

Two sets of eyes watched him go.

EMMA WEBSTER IS ABOUT TO BE OFF THE MARKET AGAIN

He loves me. He loves me not. He loves me. He loves me not. He loves me. He loves me not.

Who am I kidding?

He loves me.

RHYS WILLIAMS IS A CHANGED MAN

After his first decent night's sleep in days, Rhys woke up and lumbered out of bed, neatly ignoring Gwen's stabbing foot and her murmur of 'tea… tea… tea…'

He switched on the shower, started cleaning his teeth and hunting out some clothes for the day – all without a single thought in his head. And, when he did have a thought, it was to glimpse his reflection in the mirror and think, 'Looking good, boy.'

He got out of the shower, marvelling at how that new shower gel really did leave him feeling tingling and refreshed. Gwen pottered into the bathroom, started cleaning her teeth and then stopped, brush motionless, foam flecking her mouth. 'Mmmkhing hell!' she managed, paste dribbling onto the floor.

'What?' asked Rhys, towelling himself down.

Gwen's eyes were wide. She pointed at him with her brush. 'You're looking… well, different, that's all, Rhys. Taller.'

Rhys shrugged. 'A bit of attention from another woman, that's all it takes for you to see what you've got, love.'

'Ha. Ha,' muttered Gwen. She was knackered. Jack was right. She hadn't had a decent night's sleep this week.

'Hey, love, I reckon I've lost a bit after all, you know. I swear these jeans are hanging off me.' He stood proudly in front of her, thumb pulling out the spare fabric.

'They stretch, you know,' muttered Gwen, without really looking. And then she really looked. 'Where did you get that six pack?'

'What?' And then Rhys looked in the mirror. And a grin lit up his face. 'Bloody hell, love! I'm staying at home today and washing the car. Topless.'

Gwen narrowed her eyes. Bless Rhys. Last time he lost weight, he'd been infected with an alien parasite. This time – well, she wasn't inclined to believe that doughnuts and risotto were the magical keys to unlocking abdominal strength.

'Well done, love,' she said, keeping the worry out of her voice. Rhys seemed taller, broader – and even his face was a bit different. Slightly... well, more like he'd look in the movie of his life.

She looked at him stood there, hands on his hips, grinning at his reflection in the mirror. 'Bloody marvellous, this! I look perfect!'

As she went to put the kettle on, she noticed his grey hairs were gone and really, really started to worry.

IANTO MISSES POCKETS

They were sat in the Torchwood SUV. A traffic warden was coming towards them across the car park. Jack was sat humming quietly to himself. Gwen realised, sadly, that the man had no real idea what 'Pay and Display' actually meant.

'Ianto, hun, could you go and feed the meter? Quickly.'

'Sure,' said Ianto, and hefted something onto his lap the size of a labrador with handles. It appeared to be the world's largest handbag. He dived into it muttering, 'I'm sure I've got a purse in here somewhere.'

Gwen stifled a laugh. 'Oh, no one needs a bag that large!'

Ianto looked up, puzzled. 'But, I needed something big enough for my gun. And my house keys, and my MP3, and the phone, the PDA, the chargers, and a copy of *Captain Corelli*. Honestly, by the time you slip in some mints and a spare pair of tights, it's full house, I can tell you.'

Jack arched an eyebrow.

The traffic warden tapped on the windscreen.

Jack held up his Torchwood ID. The traffic warden shook his head.

Jack looked back, placatingly, and started fishing around in his pockets. 'Honestly, we save this city from alien disaster several times a year, and they still make us adhere to parking regulations. Do you know who really developed the internal combustion engine? Torchwood did. And this is the thanks we get. Well, that and one-way systems – the product of a tiny mind.' Jack pouted, looking for all the world like a spoiled child. It was at moments like this, those rare moments when little things didn't go Jack's way, that Gwen saw the true hero. A man not frightened by vast evil, corrupt states or lost souls, but baffled by pettiness, bureaucracy and muddling mediocrity. Why he had sentenced himself to Wales, she would never really understand.

They were parked outside Rhys's work.

That morning, Gwen had stormed into Torchwood, magnificently worried.

'My husband's too pretty!' she'd yelled. 'You've got to do something, Jack!' She caught the look in his eye. 'Don't you go sassing me, Harkness. I am deadly serious.'

'Sass?' tutted Jack in mock affront. 'I don't do sass, do I? I prefer to think of it as kittenish charm. What do you think, Ianto?'

'Definitely kittenish,' said Ianto.

'Sod the kittens,' Gwen was in full flow. 'Rhys woke up bloody gorgeous this morning, and I want to find the woman who's done that to him.'

As she spoke, she was flinging photos from her phone up onto the Hub's screens, until pictures of Rhys bobbed across the wall. Some were of their wedding, two were before and after shots of the back of his head, and one was of him this morning, wearing only a towel and waving sheepishly at the camera.

'Look at Rhys!' Gwen shrieked. 'Overnight he's gained an extra two inches!'

Jack carefully didn't say anything. Ianto examined the intricate walnut inlay of the table surface.

Gwen pressed on. 'It's not natural. It's wrong, that's what it is. He goes on a date with a supermodel. He wakes up the next day all Abercrumpet. Shortly after Ianto wakes up bloody gorgeous. Buzzz! I rather do think there just may be a link.'

She suddenly knew she had Jack's full attention. Finally.

'Emma Webster. This woman is speed-dating, Jack. She is combing through Cardiff's singletons – those she likes get a free makeover, those she doesn't end up dead. Whatever she's using, whatever her power, it's not been around more than a week. She's got her hands on some alien thing and… and… she's using it to make her ideal man.'

'Rhys?' said Ianto and Jack.

They looked again at the picture of the jovial, weakly smiling bloke drifting across the walls of their boardroom.

GWEN IS THE GREEN-EYED MONSTER

'Oh, hi, Gwen,' said Large Mandy from the office, laughing her normal large laugh. 'Are you here for Rhys? He's just on the phone. Would you like a doughnut?'

Gwen glanced at the plate full of pastries. Mandy was obviously Rhys's enabler, keeping him fuelled on whatever crap she could lay her hands on. Ah well. She wondered how Mandy had taken Rhys's sudden transformation. And then she found out.

'I must say, Gwen, love, he's looking knockout today. The girls from upstairs have been popping down to have a peek. He's quite something – I'll say this, married life suits him. Not like my Ted. Oh, I tell you, you wouldn't believe the size of him these days. I always tells people I work in haulage and they looks at Ted and they laughs. It's our little joke, see.' Mandy laughed. 'I'm glad we lives in a bungalow these days, or lord alone knows how I'd get him up and down the stairs.'

'Right,' said Gwen. This was about all she could ever think to say to Mandy.

Rhys popped his head round the door. 'Gwen? I thought it was you.'

He looked really happy to see her. Actually, he looked bloody stunning. It was ages since she'd seen him look this happy.

'Come in, come in – I've got things to tell you. It's about... Her!'

She wandered into his office, watching as he excitedly shut the cheap, thin door. She imagined Mandy on thundering tiptoe sneaking closer to eavesdrop on the other side. She clearly wasn't alone in this – Rhys had dropped his voice to a spy movie whisper.

'She! Phoned! Emma!'

'When?'

'Just now! Asking me out on a proper date!' Rhys was actually rubbing his hands together.

'Congratulations. You going to tell her you're married?'

'No! I'm going to go on the date.'

'Rhys are you out of your tiny skull? For all we know that woman is a crazed killer. Look what she's done to you already...'

Rhys looked down at himself and flashed her the same proud, silly smile he normally saved for when he let one off in the car. 'Oh, I dunno. I don't think it can be her. She's so nice, love, but this is just careful eating.'

Gwen glanced bitterly at the half-eaten doughnut on a plate by the phone. 'Bollocks. That woman is dangerous, she is manipulative, and she is after you. You are not going on that date.'

'She's hardly the black widow, is she?'

'Rhys, wherever she goes, corpses turn up. She's sliced through the dating scene in Cardiff. And now she's sunk her claws into you. She is dangerous.'

'And she's expecting me to pick her up tonight at eight. And I'm going.'

'What?'

Rhys's stubborn streak was showing. 'You want to find out more about her? You will. You can put a wire on me, you can all follow me. Dinner with her? She'll open up to the Williams charm, tell me everything about her, and you can all listen in. If she is the Black Widow of the Bay, then you can arrest her. If she's just a lonely gorgeous soul, then I'll do my best to let her down gently.'

Let her down gently? 'Oh, I'm sure she'll cope.'

'You are so jealous!' Rhys appeared delighted at this. 'It's fine. Admit it, Gwen – I'm your best lead. And isn't it just nicer to have a friendly chat over a bottle of wine than hosing her down in your cells? I won't let anything happen to me. And at the slightest sound of danger, you and Jack can come crashing in like cowboys and save me.'

'Too bloody right we will.'

'Do I get a code word?'

'Cocktail sausage. Work it into conversation however you will.'

'Can't it be saveloy?'

Gwen hugged him. 'I love you, but I think this is really, really silly. I don't want you coming to any harm.'

Rhys shook his head. 'You always were a terrible judge of women. Emma's a nice girl. And this is a first date. Nothing ever happens on a first date.'

Gwen stared at him, open-jawed. 'If she doesn't kill you, I will.'

EMMA WEBSTER IS DETERMINED

'I will not end up a gin-addled spinster in a cat-soaked attic.'

She scanned down Facebook and noticed that her ex, Paul, had changed his relationship status. She felt cold and unhappy. She'd always thought that, you know, maybe at some point they'd get back together. But here he was 'in a relationship with Helen Corrigan'. There was even a picture of the two of them out together. She looked bright and young and happy and a bit on the drunk side. He looked as good as he'd ever looked. And underneath it, he'd posted: 'Hey babe! I can't believe it – the one time I look better than you in a photo, and I'm SLAUGHTERED!!!'

Helen had commented: 'LOL!'

Emma took against her purely on that basis.

Hey, Emo girl, why so sad?

I'm just – you know, grieving for what's lost.

Grieving? The past is where you dump things you no longer need. The future's all fresh and tidy. Listen to me – we're going to do better than Paul. You're seeing Rhys tonight, aren't you? That's something to look forward to.

Emma watched as Vile Kate pottered across the office and perched on the edge of her desk, leaning over to talk to Susan.

Her mouth was starting to swell up due to some 'mystery allergy'. Despite her nastily swollen lips, she had a happy little smile on her face.

And... oh yes, a little belly. She's ballooned already! I wonder if she's noticed that everyone thinks she's pregnant. They're even getting up a card for her.

Kate finished talking to Susan about something to do with the laser printer and turned to Emma, wearing her 'sad face', even sadder due to her dramatically bloated lips that made her look like a goldfish dealing with terrible news. 'Ooh. Sorry to see your ex has found someone else. Are you OK?' She squeezed her shoulder, and Emma cursed that she'd been unable to think of a reason for declining Kate's friendship request – which gave her instant access to a treasure trove of embarrassing facts and moments.

Emma nodded. 'I've moved on.'

Kate slid her head onto one side, like she was listening for an approaching train. 'Oh. I'm so pleased. I always think it's tragic when we can't move on. There's no point in torturing yourself over your failures, pet.' And she smiled again and walked away.

Cancer?

OWEN HARPER IS STILL DEAD

Jack sat on his own in the Boardroom, just listening to the sounds of Torchwood. It was never quiet, even here, several storeys below Cardiff Bay. There was always the rumble of traffic, and the thud of the waves, the not-quite-right ticking from their unique computer system, the occasional roar of a Weevil, and the angry hum of the Rift Manipulator, the only thing keeping Cardiff from being torn out of existence. Oh, plus, sometimes, he swore he could hear the chiming of a grandfather clock, but he'd never found it, or asked Ianto where it was.

This was his time, and he loved it. In his long lives, he'd only ever felt truly at home in Torchwood – the only place and time that suited him. All the noises comforted him – in an odd way, this creepy, dark place was his only friend. It let him think.

He heard a distant footfall. Ianto, he thought. He didn't say anything until he came into the room.

'Oh, hi,' said Ianto, awkwardly. He was wearing his favourite suit back from when he'd been a man. And carrying a tray of coffee. He tried out a brave smile. 'Normal service has been resumed.' He set down the tray with a bang and waited. His smile faded as his look at Jack became desperate.

'Oh, Ianto,' Jack got up and walked over to his friend, gripping him by the shoulders. 'You look ridiculous in those clothes.'

Ianto shrugged. 'What every girl wants to hear. I just felt like a change. Hoping it would jog my memory.' He poured milk into Jack's cup, stirred it and handed it to him. Jack took it, brushing his hand against Ianto's. Ianto held it, but snatched his away when Gwen came in in a waft of pastry flakes. She put down her sausage roll on the Boardroom desk, scattering more crumbs, and grabbed a coffee from the tray. Only then did she notice Ianto. She paused. 'Hum. OK. It's quite Marlene. I'll give you that.'

'Really?' said Jack. 'I think she'd be quite upset.'

'Hey!' protested Ianto, tugging unhappily at the suddenly overlong sleeves of his jacket.

Jack pressed on.

'Now, sit down. Ianto, drink some of your excellent coffee, and listen. I've got some news. News about what made you the man you are today.'

He pushed a key, and documents managed to drift onto the Boardroom computer screen. As he waved his hands in the air, various ones floated forward to fill the wall.

'This was an active file of Owen's. He was monitoring various news reports about revolutionary gene therapy. Apparently this was a therapy that wasn't available on the NHS – the makers said they'd been told by various hospitals that it was too costly. But they were claiming some success with all the usual suspects – the big C, the big A, the even bigger A, and even baldness and wrinkles. So far – so normal. There are a dozen of these stories every week in the papers. Breakthrough press releases that are never heard from again, or turn out to be flawed studies. But you know how it is – everyone wants to be perfect, to be cured. And we know that a couple of these stories have turned out to be worth Torchwood's time. And so, they're flagged.

'This one – there was something that grabbed Owen's attention. It was partly the deliberately low-key nature of the reports. As though the people behind it wanted the public to know about it, but didn't want anyone to take it seriously. Then it turns out that...' He paused. A long document floated past in very small print. '... This is the report from the NHS trust that was supposed to have looked into this treatment. It's a fake – no one has even considered using this. It's not even been through basic testing – that's all faked too. This treatment is a fake. Which isn't necessarily a problem – only there are all of these testimonies to its success. And they read wrong – they're not showing up like the fluke cures you get from placebo trials. Nor do they read like faked testimonials. No "Mrs N of Stoke-on-Trent" – these are the real things. Names, addresses, photos. All over the last two months, appearing in papers across the country, but all claiming to have received treatment in Wales. Owen thought that this was a fake cure that accidentally worked. So, we flagged it. And then, on the night you disappeared, Gwen and I were out hunting Weevils, and here you were. Alone. Cleaning the coffee filter. Same old Saturday night. And then the file noticed this, and sent you an alert.'

A small newspaper article floated to fill the screen:

HEALTHCARE ALL AT SEA FOR MIRACLE CURE

DOCTORS ARE DEMANDING to know if a miracle cure is legal, following the discovery that secret gene treatments are being offered on a Dublin to Cardiff ferry service.'

'Oh my god!' said Gwen. 'The ferry!'

The headline swum slowly across the wall.

Gwen shook her head. 'But... No one mentioned anything strange. They just seemed shocked. They literally didn't know what hit them. Everything seemed OK.'

Jack looked at her. 'Read on...'

Nicknamed the 'Hope Boat', this is an ordinary ferry service that has been offered for the last four months. Patients can join normal passengers heading to the Emerald Isle and, once the ferry is in International Waters, the apparently 'illegal, untested' treatment can be carried out.

'It's brilliant,' said Barry Truman, 48, of Minehead. 'We did some

shopping in Cardiff, some sightseeing in Dublin, and on the way back my cancer was cured. My GP had given up on me, but apparently I'm in complete remission.'

Furious NHS officials are demanding access to the Hope Boat, but the ferry company has explained that the procedure is nothing to do with them. 'We know it goes on,' explained a spokesman for the company, 'but we don't know who carries out the treatment, or even who the patients are. All we know is that there's a lot of miracle cures going on onboard, and who are we to stop that?'

Cancer specialist Oliver Feltrow disagrees: 'Terminal illness care has always been prey to so-called miracle hoaxes like this. Proper palliative care can be derailed by these claims of a total cure, leading to a tragically inevitable relapse. The really sick people are those behind this scam.'

Passengers on the ferry last weekend rallied to support the Hope Boat. 'I had no idea,' said Mr Ross Kielty, 35, of Neath. 'Fancy learning that the wife and I have been on a shopping trip while everyone around us has been cured of god knows what. No wonder they're drinking the bar dry!'

There were several photographs accompanying the article. A picture of the ferry and a few shots of passengers. They started to drift into close-up on the screen as Jack continued his narrative.

'So, the system notices this article, and flags it as being on our very doorstep. And so, as the only person in the Hub, you print out a timetable and head out. And that's not all. Look...'

Gwen gasped. There, at the very back of a crowd of a picture from over a week ago, was a woman who looked exactly like Ianto.

'I don't remember, I don't remember,' said Ianto very quietly.

IANTO CAN RIDE A HORSE ACROSS A BEACH WITHOUT FEAR OR SHAME

'You OK?' asked Jack. Ianto was in the tourist office, diligently tidying away leaflets in the carousel. He hadn't exactly run out of the Boardroom, but it hadn't been a slow saunter either.

'No, Jack,' sighed Ianto. 'I'm really, really scared, and I don't remember a thing about that ferry. If that's not me, who is it?'

'Ianto, relax.' Jack's voice was soothing. 'Come on. Let's talk about this. See what we can sort out.'

'No,' said Ianto. 'I can't relax. My breasts really ache.' He popped down a small pile of postcards of interesting Welsh political buildings and rubbed at his left breast. 'It's really sore.'

'Would you like me to rub it better?' Jack was always smooth.

Ianto glanced sharply at him. 'Jack, it really itches. Maybe it's this top. I swear it's a poly-cotton mix, but the label says no. But then what kind of fool trusts a label? "Dry clean only"! I wasn't born yesterday.'

'You are such a princess.'

'Well yes, obviously.' Ianto was lost in thought. 'Geranium leaves are supposed to be good. But that's for when you're lactating, I think.'

'Are you lactating?' Jack wore an expression of dangerous interest.

'I assure you, you would be the last person to know if I was.' Ianto moved into a corner.

'Is that what's been different about the coffee?' Jack laughed.

Ianto snapped the elastic band off of a new batch of leaflets about an organic jam activity centre. He pinged the band expertly at Jack's ear. The Captain clapped his hands over the ear and gave Ianto a pout.

'God, you're moody these days – you're not… at that time of the month, are you?'

Ianto stared at him, horrified. 'Oh. I hope not. Am I? How can I tell?'

'Wikipedia,' Jack tutted. 'Wikipedia.'

'It's just… Look, can we sort this out before I have to find out?'

Jack reached across the desk and took Ianto's hand. He led him gently back into the Hub. 'Come on. Ianto – that ferry. What if you were on it? Gwen's going through the files, seeing if there's any reference to you. Think. Has it triggered anything? Is that little pill working?'

Ianto shrugged. 'Not really. Well, it is, kind of. I've been remembering working at a supermarket while I was at university. I can remember the prices of everything. From tinned peas to cereals. Every single brand. It's not terribly helpful, but it's allowed me to work out the true rate of inflation.'

'Can you remember anything more? Think. Ferry. Ever been on the ferry before?'

Ianto shook his head. 'No. The only time I took the Irish ferry was from Swansea when I was a kid. Mum drank two pints of Guinness on the way over and was sick and she clipped me over the ear when I laughed.'

'Thank you. That's charming, but not entirely helpful.'

'It was cold and windy, and they only had Panda Cola and I wanted a slush puppy.' Ianto's face took on a wistful glaze. 'And… ah.' His face lit up. 'The full range of alcopops and a quite unbelievable offer on cocktail jugs. But I'm travelling on my own, and I don't like saying the names out loud.' He stole a glance at Jack. 'Some of them are quite frank, you know.'

'That they are. People who order Sex On A Beach have clearly never done it.' Jack cupped a hand to Ianto's cheek. 'Well done, Ianto. We've a recent memory. Anything more?' Jack had steered him down to the Boardroom. He signalled Gwen over.

Ianto's eyes started to cloud over just slightly, and a thought happened. 'I'm starting to remember something. Oh yes.'

'What?'

Ianto shuddered. 'Hen night.'

2. LUCKY DEBBIE'S DUTY-FREE PURSUIT OF LOVE

IANTO IS HAVING A FLASHBACK

It is last Friday night. Ianto is on a ferry. Ianto is alone at the bar. Ianto is a man. Which, at the time, isn't surprising, really. But thinking about it now… Anyway, he's there on the ferry, pulling out of Cardiff Bay, and there's a little cabin with orange curtains and a stranger snoring in the top bunk, so he's at the bar. He's asked them to make him a coffee to keep him alert, and he's not liking any of it. The beans were burnt, over-diluted, and it's been sat in the coffee-maker since February. He thinks he may stop being so silly. He's supposed to blend in, but here he is at the bar in a suit drinking coffee from a tiny cup and saucer and all around him is noise and formica and laughter and music from every nightmare wedding disco in his life.

He's keeping an eye out. Someone here. Several someones. Someone must be a patient. Someone must be ill. Does anyone look ill? Or out of place? Who are the patients? Who are the doctors? There's a hen night over there, dressed as nurses, but they've also got on devil horns, angel wings and some tinsel. Perhaps it's all a double bluff? Ah. Cunning.

He looks over at them a bit more. They seem happy and very drunk. They're all so young and so loud and keep yelling out for Lucky Debbie. He guesses Debbie is getting married.

'Hello, sailor!' says a voice at his elbow.

He looks around. She's quite drunk but very pretty. And wearing L-Plates.

'Hello.' He smiles.

'I'm Debbie,' she says. She's trying to attract the attention of the bored bar staff by waving a handful of notes.

'As in Lucky Debbie?'

She smiles. 'Yeah. And you?'

'Ianto. Not lucky at all, really.'

She makes a boo-hoo face at him. 'Well, we can change all that, you know. Clearly, I'm spoken for – not that that's gonna stop me licking whipped cream off the nipples of a Chippendale tomorrow night – but lots of my friends are... well, you know... Hen Night. Come on, join us. Hey!' This to a barman, who appears to be twelve and entirely covered in acne. 'Four jugs of Screaming Orgasm, One Shitting Whippet, a rack of Zambucas and a pineapple juice.'

'Pineapple juice?' asks Ianto.

Debbie leans forward, a bit confidential. 'There's a reason why I'm Lucky Debbie. And a lot of it's to do with pacing myself when I'm around those screaming whores. God, we have a laugh, but sometimes it all gets a bit much. And when you've picked vomit out of your hair on the bus home once, it's kind of... a sign. You want anything?'

'I can be tempted.'

'Oh, then you'll love my friend Kerry. She's quite formidable when you first meet, but easier than a GCSE.'

'Ah. I see. Um. Just a diet coke please.'

Debbie laughs. 'Seriously? The booze is dead cheap on here. It's not like flying.'

'I know,' says Ianto. 'But, I'll let you in on a thing. I'm a secret agent for an organisation that's beyond the Government, above the UN. And I'm on a mission. So I'm not drinking, see.'

Lucky Debbie's eyes wander away erratically, watching the

barman pour skimmed milk over a jugful of ice. The sound system starts to play 'You're Beautiful'.

'Awww...' says Debbie. 'I hate this song. But love it at the same time. You know what I mean? Like, I can't stand hearing it, but I would love someone to sing it to me. I tried explaining this to Phil. My Phil. Lucky Phil, if you like. But he thought I was asking him to do Karaoke. Sad, really. You know what I mean?'

Ianto nods, sipping gratefully at his drink. 'I dunno,' he says eventually. 'I've always had time for sincere music.'

Debbie tilts her head on one side. 'Yeah,' she says. 'Help us carry over these drinks and join in the party. With that suit they'll think you're a stripper.'

'Why thank you,' says Ianto.

Ianto doesn't know it yet, but he is being watched. He's trying to blend in, he's trying not to arouse suspicion, but he is. He noticed that there were two people standing in the shadows of the dock as he got aboard the boat. There was something odd about them. Two men, dressed like sailors out of a perfume commercial, just standing and watching people get on the ferry, smiling blankly.

Oddly, it's not them who are watching him.

Later, Ianto is sat at a table in the ferry bar. He's quiet, but he's watching the room. Around him are the girls. Including Kerry, who keeps giggling and nudging his arm, which just makes Ianto feel a bit bashful. He's sipping his drink, and he's watching the girls. They're having fun. Simple, really drunken fun. It's been ages since he's done this. He's feeling a bit... not left out. Just... sad.

He remembers the last time he went for an evening out. Tosh got tiddly and danced like a dervish. Owen tried not to break anything coming back from the bar with drinks. Gwen was laughing cos she'd recognised her first boyfriend from school

('Bloody hell, he's gone bald!'), and Jack – Jack had looked at everyone else in the room then suddenly, on a whim, turned to him and smiled the widest smile in the world. Then Tosh came staggering over, laughing out loud at the word 'Kajagoogoo'. She tugged at his elbow, insisted he dance.

But Tosh is gone now, and there's Kerry.

The bar staff are bringing more drinks to the table, somehow managing to keep the tray stable while the room tilts from side to side.

Ianto isn't feeling sick, which he finds remarkable. And Kerry keeps asking if he wants to dance. He carries on observing the room. An old couple come in and take a glass of wine each to a small table. He watches them. They're a possibility. There's another man sitting alone – he's wearing a terrible jumper and drinking beer from a jug, so possibly Norwegian.

The girls all start to sing along to the music. Ianto thinks, 'I may be undercover, but no. There are some things I cannot do.' So, after a wan smile, he leaves them to sing about their umbrella.

The cold night air really, really clears his head. He takes a walk around, heading down a flight of stairs and into a long corridor. It's quite an old ship and there's a lot of it that's like his childhood – full of browns and oranges and formica. There are lots of narrow passages. It's an old Norwegian ferry, and so there are signs scattered around in English, Norwegian (he guesses) and Welsh. Apart from the bar staff, the crew are spookily absent, so there's no one to go up to and ask, 'Excuse me, have you seen any alien technology?'

He passes a few doors marked 'Staff Only'. But they're not locked, and just lead to boring corridors without even lino. The ship is lurching alarmingly, and Ianto is finally feeling a bit sick. He can sense the sweat pricking under his clothes. He makes his way to a railing and breathes, breathes, breathes.

He's got a night on the boat, a day in Dublin, and then a trip back. What if it's all like this? It's oddly like an airport departure lounge at sea. Completely anonymous, faceless, the perfect cover. Everyone's a stranger, everyone's nobody.

He passes a sign advertising events on the ship. It is, gloriously, an old-fashioned velveteen board onto which little gold block letters have been pinned haphazardly. It tells him that there'll be some poker in a function room. It mentions that there's a small private party for someone's wedding. It welcomes a car dealership who are on a trip. And it says that the cinema, in addition to screening some films from last year, will be showing a 'health presentation' in an hour's time.

'Health presentation?' Bingo.

Back in the bar, appearing normal, Ianto sits down next to Lucky Debbie. She's singing merrily away, and pats him on the arm. 'You're gorgeous,' she says. 'Kerry really likes you.' She laughs, her breath rich with alcopop. She digs him in the arm. 'You can get a snog, cheer you up. Cure the seasick!'

'Can I?' Ianto says, trying to sound enthusiastic. Kerry appears to be asleep at the table, slumped face down in a cake, the tinsel from her angel wings hanging loose in the breeze.

'Yeah – when she wakes up. Bless 'er. I'm having a great night. Are you?'

'Yes. Yes I am, thank you.' Actually, yes, I am. Hmm.

'Why are you on the boat? Business trip? A lonely travelling salesman?'

Ianto shakes his head. 'No. Like I said – I'm a secret agent.'

Lucky Debbie barks with laughter and clinks his glass. 'You're full of it. Bless, what are you like?'

'Well…' Ianto demurs. 'I did see that there's a seminar on health in the cinema in a bit.'

Debbie makes an exaggerated yawn. 'Right. And any minute now we've got a stripper booked if Kerry's organised it right. What'd you rather see? A film about vitamins, or an oiled stranger stirring your pint with his tackle?'

Ianto considers. 'Well, when you put it like that, I'd better just pop along and watch my vitamin film.'

Debbie laughs and nudges him on the shoulder. 'Stay a bit more, eh? Who knows – Kerry may come round for a bit. Just one more pineapple juice. Stay…'

Ianto checks his watch.

Ianto walks into the cinema as the ship lurches quite alarmingly. He clutches at an old flip-down chair. He manages not to spill any popcorn as he sits down. He suspects that, just slightly, he might appear drunk and harmless. Or, as his auntie used to say, 'tiddly'. Good.

He sneaks a look around himself. There are a clutch of people in the cinema, which has thin carpets thick with chewing gum and a pervasive, cabbagey smell of popcorn. There is an old couple in a corner. They have brought notepads. There is a bored-looking girl in the second row.

A single man, very thin and quite yellow, is sat on his own, coughing slightly. A little away from him is a bald, fat, middle-aged man listening to an iPod and laughing a bit too loudly.

Projected onto the screen are a series of slides advertising amenities on board, special offers at the bar, and a range of interesting snacks available. Music is playing (the theme from *Van Der Valk*, on pan-pipes). There is an atmosphere of comfortable anticipation. He notices the old couple keep squeezing each other's hands and bickering quietly. They remind him of his parents – perfectly content in each other's company, passing the days in a series of complicated little arguments and score-settlings. The old lady reaches over and adjusts her husband's shirt collar. She looks like the kind of woman ready to pounce on grandchildren with spittle and a tissue at the slightest hint of a stain. Ianto decides he likes them. What treatment are they here for?

He decides the thin, yellow man is dying – probably of about five different things. Perhaps the oldies were just becoming forgetful, or hoping to keep rowing for a few more years. Perhaps the bored girl had just wandered in. The bald, fat man might be looking to lose weight and gain hair. Who knew?

But what about himself? Ianto tries to think of something important he could be in need of curing. Perhaps he could just claim curiosity.

Van Der Valk fades away and the slide of the Balti Buffet chunks off. There is a blue screen, a fizzing, and then, of all wonders, an old VHS tape projects into life. The picture crackles, crackles, wobbles and then slow tracking snow drifts down the screen. With an abrupt final crackle, the feature starts. For a brief instant, Ianto is in darkness and about to see Indiana Jones with his father sat on his right, a small bucket of popcorn balanced between them and an orange ice lolly melting stickily over his knuckles.

The picture goes white, and a reassuring logo of cupped hands rising up around a globe appears. Synthesised music swells out, a tune of energy and warmth that sounds just like (and yet, for copyright reasons completely unlike) the theme from *Top Gear*.

A smooth voice pours over shots that track across an empty hospital ward, a crowded waiting room, and then through a garden where people of all ages walk in the sun. The tone is warm, upbeat and strident.

'Welcome to Hope. We've got used to living in an age of miracles. Where the cure for everything is just around the corner. But what if you can't wait until tomorrow? Well, we're here to tell you about how we can offer you the medicine of tomorrow today. This is not a trial. This is not a placebo. This is real hope, a real cure – the stuff of dreams. What we are offering on this boat is not legal, but it is moral. We refuse to keep back a cure that works. This is not alternative therapy, homeopathy, or moonshine – this is the real thing. We've worked on a genetic therapy that offers real, rapid repairs of your DNA…'

At this point the screen moves from sunsets and a hopeful woman boiling a kettle while staring wistfully out of her kitchen window to exciting computer graphics of spinning molecules and then some science stuff of cells dividing. Ianto frowns, and sneaks a glance around the cinema. He was right – someone's come in. Standing at the back of the room are a man and a woman. Both of them startlingly good looking. They exude health, prosperity and well-being. Their arms are linked and they stand watching the screen with rapt, smiling attention. Ianto recognises the woman from the newspaper article. He immediately decides they are involved. The woman catches his glance and smiles at him. Ianto does what he always does when a beautiful woman smiles at him across a room. He blushes and looks away and feels about fourteen.

'… Our swift, non-invasive procedure is over in minutes, has no side effects, and the difference can be felt at once. We offer this treatment here on the Hope Boat as it is illegal in Britain. Rejected by the NHS as impossible to test and too expensive, we are only too happy to offer it here, in international waters. Simply sign up after this seminar, and a visit will be made to your cabin in the morning. Then, you can relax and enjoy a day's sightseeing on the Emerald Isle, followed by a revolutionary cure on the voyage back to Cardiff. It's that easy. And this treatment can work on all sorts of genetic ailments – from simple male-pattern baldness all the way through to cancer. We can make you better. No,' a warm smile in the voice, 'we *will* make you better.'

The picture changes to a warmly setting sun watched by a couple on a beach. And then fades to black.

The lights come on, together with a slide advertising the wide range of gnomes available in the duty-free shop. People stand up. The old couple look at each other, and squeeze each other's hands. The beautiful people at the back have already left.

'Well,' thinks Ianto, munching on his cold popcorn, 'that was the fishiest thing in the Irish Sea.'

'And then?' asked Gwen.

'I signed up, and had a lovely day sightseeing,' said Ianto. 'I think I took loads of photos on my phone. The weather was a bit drab, but the girls were great fun.'

'The girls? Lucky Debbie and Easy Kerry.' Jack's mockery was fond and only a little bit jealous. 'Let me guess. You went drinking?'

Ianto shook his head. 'Actually, we went to the zoo, a nice little tea shop, and Kerry found some rare editions she'd been hunting after for ages in an antiquarian bookstore.'

It's late afternoon in a Dublin pub with a great view of the rain. Ianto reels. Lucky Debbie grabs hold of him. 'Easy, tiger!' She ruffles his hair and helps him sit down. All around him, the wooden panels of the Dublin bar start to spin slowly.

Ianto shakes his head, and scowls. 'I'm tired.' He is much drunker than he intended to be.

Debbie grins and pinches his cheek. 'You pass out, and Kerry will pounce. I've experience of that girl. Don't give in to weakness.'

Ianto runs a hand through his hair. 'Debbie, I'm hammered. I'm trying to do really important work here, and my head's pounding. I have no idea what was in the meal we've just eaten, but three fingers of scotch aren't helping anything. I just want a nap.'

Kerry staggers back from the ladies, giggling. There is a small trail of toilet paper stuck to the bottom of her shoe. She sits down opposite Ianto with a *whumpf!* and then pitches gently into an uneasy sleep on an open packet of pork scratchings.

Ianto squints a little to bring the table into focus. Spread across it are the slumbering remains of Debbie's hen party. Through a forest of half-finished pints and abandoned pies he can see Debbie, who winks at him. 'You'll be fine, doll. What is this top secret mishun? You really a spy?'

Ianto shakes his head. 'Oh no. I'm just the office boy, really. But… you know… I'm keeping an eye out. For a friend. Well, not really a friend – more a bastard, really. But he died. And it's easy to remember someone fondly if they're dead. Especially when they died twice, if you're counting. Twice dead bastard.' He giggles.

Debbie is nodding with the slightly glassy look of someone who isn't even listening.

Ianto ventures on. 'And Owen thought there was something wrong about the boat. And he was right – I think there's some alien medical procedure taking place on that boat. And that's never good. And I'm supposed to stay sober on a mission. But then I think I'm being followed. So, I decide to blend in by getting drunk with you. Which may not have been the wisest thing. So it's Ianto Jones, secret agent, saving the Cardiff Ferry from an alien invasion, just a little bit legless. So yes, I guess in many ways it's oh dear.' He takes an ill-advised swig of his pint and grimaces. 'Oh, this is going down like sick.' He rests the glass on the table hurriedly. 'Anyway – I'm very important. I'm saving Cardiff.'

Debbie nods again and pats his hand. 'Phil was shagging Kerry a couple of months ago,' she says, quietly.

Many hours later, they stagger onto the boat for the journey back. Kerry is throwing up into a bin to the disgust of customs officials. Debbie has a spring in her step and flashing plastic devil horns in her hair. Ianto is carrying a traffic cone.

He makes it back to his tiny little orange cabin and slumps down on the lower bunk, the traffic cone resting unsteadily by him. He sinks his head in his hands. 'I am so hammered,' he thinks sadly. 'I've had a brilliant weekend, clearly. I haven't let my hair down in ages. But I haven't really saved the world.'

He wraps his arms round the traffic cone, and settles down for a sleep. At no point does he even notice the envelope resting on the floor.

The knock on the door wakes him. It is night and the throbbing of the engines pounds in his head. 'Whu?' he manages, unsteadily getting to his feet. He is praying it isn't Debbie. Or, dear god forbid, Kerry.

Instead it is a small, dapper little man in a steward's uniform. He has a drooping orange moustache that makes him look pleasantly like Asterix. 'Sir,' says the man with the perfect English of a Norwegian. 'You are awaited in the Kielty cabin.'

'Ah,' says Ianto. 'Thank you. Do you mind if I…?' He gestures to the sink, where he splashes some cold water on his face and straightens his tie. Oh god, he feels awful. He grabs the complimentary bottle of water from the washstand and starts to drink it as they walk. His mouth tastes terrible as though… oh no. Has he been smoking? He really can't remember. Lisa will kill him.

As they walk his brain does three bits of thinking. The first pieces of thinking it has done for almost twenty-four hours. The first thought is 'Kielty' – the name was mentioned in the newspaper story. Ross Kielty had apparently been a passenger, and spoke in glowing terms of the treatment. In the same article… something else familiar. The picture. He'd seen someone else in the picture. He tries to remember who. But it now seems obvious that the whole Hope Boat is an elaborate cover for something else.

The steward leads him to a door and then melts away. Ianto sadly swallows the last of the bottled water and knocks. A quite beautiful woman opens the door and smiles kindly.

'Mr Jones?' she says, holding out her hand. Her handshake is easy and strong. 'Thank you for coming. My name is Christine. Do take a seat.'

He steps into the cabin – which seems to be the ferry's equivalent of a stateroom. It is still the size of a small caravan, but feels almost palatial.

The woman, amazingly dressed and terribly calm, sits down opposite him, and smiles. She is half of the couple who had come into the cinema late. She is professionally friendly. 'Now, briefly tell me what can we do for you?'

'Ah,' says Ianto. 'Can you cure my hangover?'

Christine's laugh is a sharp little rattle. 'Oh, we can cure a lot more than that, Mr Jones. What was it that you came to see us about? Surely something more serious?'

Ianto sighs. 'I don't know. I read about the treatments offered on this boat, and I wondered… well. You see, in the last year I've lost my girlfriend and two friends. They all died. And everyone thinks very sad, but move on. But I can't. I'll be at work, and I'll remember a conversation I had with her, or a row with Owen, just a little thing, and I'll be stuck. I want that to stop. I know you can cure my body – but can you cure my mind? Can you make it so that I never think about any of them ever again?'

Christine reaches out a hand that brushes his lightly. Her smile is wan and melancholy. 'Oh, Mr Jones. I'm sorry for your loss… deeply and sincerely so.' A heavy breath, and then more warmth in the smile. 'But you'll be pleased to hear that we *can* help.'

'Really?' Ianto, just for an instant, thinks how nice it would be – never to think about Lisa back in his flat. To be able to water Owen's plants without remembering him. Or dismantling Tosh's complicated analyses of alien technology – studies that would never be finished, secrets that would never be unlocked. Just forget about them and move on.

Christine leans forward. 'It won't take long, and I promise it won't hurt.'

'Will it be now?'

She taps his wrist again. 'So eager! But no – we prefer to have a pre-treatment meeting. Just to screen people, to make sure they're really happy to take part and that they understand everything. And, also, there is the small matter of payment up front.' Her smile assures him that, if it were up to her, there wouldn't be such a thing as payment.

'Oh, of course!' Ianto has the bank details of a Torchwood holding account. He passes them over, and she hands him a little slip of paper, discreetly folded in half. He lifts it up, and looks at the amount.

For a second he forgets how tired and drunk he is and instead stares aghast at the figure on the slip of paper. These people could clearly charge anything they wanted. He guesses running a ferry as a disguise can't come cheap. But still – this is…

He manages a rueful smile. 'It'll be worth it in the long run.'

'Of course,' Christine lays a reassuring hand around his shoulder. 'Once these bank details have cleared, we'll contact you later tonight with a slot for treatment. It should only take a quarter of an hour. Shouldn't hold up your fun with the hen party!' She nudges his arm and laughs warmly. Ianto returns her smile weakly. She's just confirmed that he's been watched closely ever since he got on the ship.

'What do you use?' he asks, suddenly.

Christine doesn't even look startled. Her voice has an easy, practised flow to it.

'There are various advanced gene therapies that have been developed which, for one reason or another, just aren't ever going to be practical for conventional medical care to offer. Too expensive for the NHS, impossible to obtain through other channels. My husband and I have found a way of making these therapies available easily. We use a method of delivery that's tailored to each subject. Our primary concerns are your health and well-being. We wouldn't proceed if there was any risk to you, or any chance of the procedure failing. You are in safe hands.'

'Well,' thinks Ianto. 'That was all guff. Deliberately reassuring flannel.'

He makes a face. 'But are there any injections? I've always hated those.'

Christine nods. 'Oh, me too! But rest assured – this is far less invasive and far more effective. We don't even need to give you an anaesthetic. Less fuss than a filling. Can you believe it?'

Right, thought Ianto. That does it – they've definitely nicked something alien. Miracle alien cures are never good.

He tries to leave her cabin without looking furtive and strides down the corridor, fingering his phone. No signal. He waits round the corner and then, when all is quiet, slips past Christine's cabin to the one next door, and listens quietly at the door. He can hear a man's soothing tones and a woman crying quietly. He stands back in the shadows and waits.

Eventually the door opens, and the very handsome man who'd been with Christine stands on the threshold, ushering two figures out. It is the old couple he'd noticed earlier. They are clasping each other and smiling. The old woman has tears running down her smiling cheeks.

'Now, you've nothing to worry about – just go and have a nice little lie-down, and by the time we pull in to harbour, you should notice some dramatic improvements. Just relax and feel the Parkinson's melt away. No, don't thank me any more – just settle back and enjoy the next few years together.'

The woman turns and grips Ross Kielty in a fierce embrace. She starts to cry again. Her husband gently takes her shoulders and leads her away. Ianto can hear them laughing as they walk off.

Ross stands on the threshold, smiling. He is holding something small and blue in his hands. And then turns back into the room and closes the door.

Curing Parkinson's? Oh dear.

Ianto is nervous on the deck. There's a chill in the air and he's not sure if he's been followed. But there is definitely something up. He walks towards the bar and can see people spilling out of it onto the deck. He can still hear little gusts of music from the bar as people push through the doors. Everyone is standing, looking out to sea, or pointing vaguely with their camera phones.

He glances out, trying to see what they can see – and all he notices is the distant, distant glow of Cardiff, and then higher up, a dancing spot of light, like a shooting star, but one that slices across the sky towards them, only to vanish momentarily before sparkling up again.

'It's the Northern Lights!' he hears someone shout, only to hear them laughed down. Gradually, with muttering, gasping, camera snapping and moaning they realise that the boat is surrounded by a perfect circle of fog, a fog that blots out Cardiff and the stars, just leaving a little twinkling globe that flickers closer and closer. There is nervous excitement, a definite feeling of anticipation. Ianto has no idea what the light is – he just knows it is linked to whatever is in the cabin, and the mysterious figures he saw in the Bay before he left. This is it. He reaches for his phone. Still no signal. And then, with a sputter, no battery.

He looks out across the deck, as the little twinkling fireflies of camera phones snuff out one by one.

Oh god. No witnesses.

The light comes closer and closer.

At first like fireworks – a bright ball of light arcs twice over the boat. Then Lucky Debbie runs up and grabs Ianto's hand. 'It's still! The sea!' she hisses. All around them, the waves settle flat, bowing down like lions before the light.

Then comes the sound – a roar of an ancient horn, like the loudest, most exciting, most frightening thing Ianto has ever heard.

For a second, it is dark. Very, very dark. And utterly silent.

And then the light comes back, a giant ball that sweeps over the boat, and then, with the sounding again of that awful horn, it splits into two, two balls of fire that circle round and round the deck.

Then the horn sounds a third time. It doesn't die away, but is followed by a deep boom – the shattering thud of something tearing deep underneath the water. There are screams from all around, but Ianto barely hears them. 'Oh god,' he thinks, realising how alone they are. In the distance, he can't even see Cardiff any more. Just this fog bank. Blocking them off from the world.

Something bad is going to happen – he knows it, feeling as afraid as he felt when in trouble at school, when he went on a date knowing he was going to be dumped, or when he'd gone back into Torchwood to find Lisa. Something terrible is going to happen and there is nothing he can do to stop it. No weapons, no technology, no Toshiko, no Captain Jack. Just Ianto Jones against this.

The balls of light arc over again, and with a scream of tin, sheets of steel rip up from the deck and flutter into the sea.

The shouts from the bar are louder now, all the more so for the completely still sea. The siren wail of the horn finally fades like a wounded beast and the balls of light glow and descend, floating along the deck until they are just above the surface. Dancing inside each sphere is… a shape. And he can hear laughter.

The spheres contract, melt, each shape flowing into a human form carved out of sun. The two figures stride forward, their feet just failing to touch the ground. One turns to the other. It speaks, a voice thundering and echoing like continents slapping together.

'We are here for one thing. And those who have it know what that is.'

'Give it up!' bellows the other. 'Bring it out now.'

'Please,' the other sighs, like an avalanche.

The other stretches out a hand, and light boils across the deck, wrapping around the mast, and then whipping across the lifeboats, shattering each one in a cloud of burning splinters. People start to scream. One of the figures turns, a hand forming a gentle sssshing motion against its glowing face. The first steps forward, past Ianto. Ianto feels a warmth like a furnace flicker across his cheek. 'You have two minutes.'

A pause. Then the other figure turns and steps almost shiftily towards the passengers who bunch up against the advancing heat. It speaks, its voice lower, more discreet.

'Anyone got a fag?'

What? Ianto is moved and not surprised when Lucky Debbie steps forward, fumbling in her handbag for a Superking. The figure reaches out a hand and takes it, leaning over her. 'Thanks,' it says, its voice dropping to almost a whisper.

Somehow it holds the cigarette in its glowing fingers, and then lets the end spark into life by itself. It pauses, leaning closer, conspiratorially. 'This had better not be menthol.'

'No,' says Debbie, very quietly and firmly.

The figure takes a drag. 'Lovely. Thank you. You'll be the last to die.'

Debbie nods, but her face is set into the Swansea-girl look which says, 'You're not all that.'

The figure strides above the deck, gently smoking away, while the other rises up, expanding and pulsing dangerously.

'They've not come out.'

'No, I know that.' There's a petulant note. Almost disappointed. 'I'd expected better of them.' A long sigh that rolls out across the sea. 'Fine.' Both fists burst into giant balls of flame that lash out, smashing into the bar, scattering tables and glasses and people. There are screams and cries and the smell of burning nylon carpet.

'Do you hear us, Christine and Ross?' boom both of the

figures together, their voices louder than a storm. 'We're getting violent. People are going to die soon. You'd better not be hiding, cos we're going to put on a bloody great show.'

'You selfish pricks,' snaps the smoking figure, bitterly.

The shapes come down, floating in front of Ianto and Debbie. Ianto can feel the hiss of the air starting to boil, can see those fists split and crack out into flaming, angry spheres. He feels Debbie tense up next to him – brave up to the end. Not so Lucky Debbie, he thought sadly. Then, swallowing, he opens his mouth.

'I...' His voice vanishes.

One of the figures flashes up next to him, fire scorching Ianto's face. As it stares into him with eyes of coal, he feels his flesh begin to smoulder and burn. He cries out slightly.

'Yes?'

'I...' He finds his voice, and is saddened to hear it is a yelp. 'I know who you're looking for. I can take you to them.'

The scorching heat retreats. Ianto opens his eyes. He sees Debbie give him a look – a look that mixes hope and relief with... betrayal? He shrugs.

'Go on, then!' The figure shrinks to almost human size, and lays a hand on Ianto's shoulder. It jerks its neck at its companion. 'Come on, you.'

And Ianto heads down into the hold. Around him, he can hear the plates of the ship ticking and pinging like an old clock, and see them bulging in and out, as though somehow confining these creatures in a small space. Their presence is too big.

'Am I doing the right thing?' he thinks, stepping carefully down the corridor. On the one hand, probably not. Probably there is no right thing to do at this point. Whatever, he has the feeling people are going to die. It is just a question of how many, and why. It is the kind of awkward thing he usually leaves up to Jack. After all, if you don't really sleep, you can't have nightmares about your mistakes now, can you?

Ianto feels his face smarting and burning. He knows he'll need treatment for the wound. But he doesn't dare draw attention to it. He keeps silent, marching ahead of the two balls of energy, feeling them snap and hiss with energy like steaks on a fire.

In the distance there is a loud, dull explosion, and the ship suddenly tilts. Ianto grabs a rail before he falls back onto the creatures.

'What was that?' snaps one.

'God knows,' says the other with a laugh. 'Hardly know my own strength. I think this boat's buggered, though.'

Ianto feels a shove in his shoulders. 'Then come on. Get a move on.'

The cabin is empty, as he expects. He turns around to give an explanation, and a flaming hand slaps across his face, knocking him into the wall. He looks up to see one of the glowing figures standing over him, spitting flames.

'They were here!' he protests. 'I think your arrival might have tipped them off.'

One of the figures turns to the other, and whispered, 'See? I said – softly, softly. But no – all hallelujah and fireballs. Brilliant.'

The other hisses back. 'And? It just means we'll have to take this boat apart until we find them.' The light around him flares, and Ianto feels the air in the room become suddenly stifling. Sweating, he runs a finger around his collar.

'Look,' he says. 'There's somewhere else.'

At first, the cinema seems empty. The only lights are little twinkling halogen landing strips along the floor. As soon as the figures step in behind Ianto, the room is lit with a crackling firelight.

It makes the room look even eerier as the shadows of the chairs dance up and down across each other. The dead acoustics of the cinema wrap themselves around Ianto. All he can hear is the sound of the two walking bonfires behind him.

One of them speaks softly. 'Ross? Christine? Are you here?'

There is no answer.

It speaks again. 'Come on. You're right to be scared. We are furious. But that doesn't mean we can't be reasoned with.'

The other figure snorts derisively.

'You know we want it back. You know that it's not yours. You know that you can't control it. We can, and we'll look after it. The device is not a toy. People are going to start dying, and it'll be all your fault. Just give it back to us.'

The other figure joins in, its voice harsh. 'You know what we are. You've known us for ages. We've found you. You can try and run – but we'll only find you again. And maybe, just maybe, if you give up this time, no one will die. Come on out.'

There is a pause. Ianto suddenly senses someone near him breathing out.

With a flick of a seat, Christine stands up in the darkness, cradling something close to her chest. She looks terrified.

'Oh god,' she says.

Ianto steps towards her, but she motions him away, and walks haltingly towards the two balls of light. They flow towards her. She gestures out with no, not a gun, but the pebble thing Ianto had glimpsed earlier.

One of the figures laughs. 'Oh, it's not a weapon, Christine. It's told you that several times in the last minute, I expect. You can't make it do anything it doesn't want to do. Just give it to us, please. We can't take it from you. You know that.'

'I just want...' she begins, and then looks at Ianto. 'I'm so scared.'

'You have every right to be, Christine,' says the figure on the right. 'Just give us it back, though, and it'll all be OK. Won't it?' It turns to the other figure who doesn't speak, but nods slightly. 'See?'

They both glide closer, the flickering light casting dancing shadows across her frightened face.

'I don't want to,' says Christine, firmly, holding out an arm to ward them off.

A glowing hand shoots out, grabbing Christine's. It starts to burn instantly and she screams, but the hand doesn't move.

'See Christine?' The figure's voice is soothing. 'Can you remember when you were first burned? Was it when you were a child? And your mother ran your hand under the cold tap? What felt worse? The hot…' Suddenly the flames burn blue. 'Or the cold?'

Christine whimpers.

'Help me!' she cries to Ianto again. But Ianto can't move, can't really think.

'Where's Ross?' asks the creature. 'Where is he?'

'I don't know,' she hisses. She shakes her head, her teeth clenched. 'I lost him. I think he's run away. I would tell you – oh god. I'd tell you.' She starts to cry.

'He always did panic,' sighs the fireball. 'You married a coward, Christine. He's left you all alone. He's left you to burn.'

She shakes her head again. Ianto can smell the room. It's hot and reeks of paraffin and scalded nylon and cooking meat and burning hair.

'You're all alone.' Christine's hand is released. As Ianto watches, she staggers back, holding up her hand, suddenly healed. He blinks. He can still smell roasting pork.

And then her hand is grasped again. She screams out.

'We can carry this on. Like an old Greek torture – those broken heroes who spend eternity growing new eyes only to have vultures pluck them out again. We can do that – here in this little … hey, it is a cinema, isn't it?'

Christine nods, gasping.

'Nice. Anyway – we can keep going for hours. The burning, the healing. But you have to give it back to us. You must surrender it. And then it'll stop.'

'I can't give it up. I can't. Take it from me! Please.'

A sad shake of a burning head. 'We can't. You know we can't. If it doesn't want to go, you either have to give it up, or we take it from your body once the spirit has left it.'

Christine starts to sob uncontrollably, but the burning continues.

Ianto looks around, desperately. By trying really hard, he just moves his left foot, slightly.

'We know what will happen. The fire will tear your body apart, as fast as the device can cure you. It's frantically trying to remember how you look, even now. It's desperate to keep you perfect – but how long can it keep pumping out that perfect genetic pattern?'

The figure steps closer, its hand sliding further up her arm. Christine lets out a long wail, and starts to sink to the floor.

'Make it stop, Christine, please,' says the figure as smoke curls up from her shirt. 'This isn't how we operate. But you've stolen from us… and this is nothing to the harm you've caused already. Please.'

'No!' she screams. And she carries on screaming. And, as she turns towards Ianto, suddenly her hair catches fire. And oh god then—

He catches something. It's been thrown at him.

What the what the what the? says a voice in his head. Jack's voice?

And suddenly Ianto feels very strange.

And Ianto is running, and all around him he can sense the boat being torn apart. The shrieking of metal, the dull snapping of wood, and an alarming lurching sensation.

He is running through the car bay, rolling over and over as cars and lorries tip and spin, churning in the water like socks in a washing machine. He sees a Smart car hurled through the air, burning as it crashes against the concrete wall. Petrol pours out from it, igniting and sputtering against the water, racing towards him. He rolls down, his face smacking against the wet concrete. He catches a brief glimpse of a burning figure striding towards him, and then he is off again, running up tiny metal stairs, feeling the sting of the sea air on his face.

The boat is tumbling from side to side. He sees Lucky Debbie standing there on the deck. She is looking at him. Somehow magnificent in her nurse's uniform and L-plate and devil's horns. Trying to work out whether or not to jump into the sea. Around her cables snap in the air like whips. And then she is gone.

He knows he has to get off the boat. He knows what he has to do. And he is suddenly scrambling over the railings. He hears shouts behind him. And he jumps.

A second in the air. All cold. He looks down and the sea rushes up like a sheet of glass. And then a sharp feeling as he slices through it.

And now…

It was dark in the Boardroom. Jack and Gwen sat, looking at Ianto. He held his hand up, marvelling that it was a woman's hand. Gwen smiled at him fondly, and gave him a squeeze. Jack just looked at him, wearing that calmly interested expression.

'So,' said Ianto. 'That was all a bit of a rush, wasn't it? That's all I can remember. Oh, apart from getting stuck on a very long coach journey when I was a student.' He pouted slightly. 'And you're sure it's true?'

Gwen nodded, sadly. 'The ferry was damaged. There were quite a few survivors, but all of them were in shock. I've spent days talking to them, but it just didn't seem very Torchwood. No one's said anything about this. No one mentioned weird medicine, strange devices or talking flame. They just said the boat hit something and started to sink. Not even that much, really. They all just seemed shocked and lucky to be alive. Seems like someone altered their memories for us, which is curious.' Gwen clicked her mouse, and the passenger list swam across the wall. 'But not the passenger list. And Ross and Christine Kielty are listed as passengers.' She pulled up a couple of pictures.

'Hey, Christine,' said Jack.

Ianto looked at the picture, and nodded. 'That's me. That's her. She died. Burning like a candle. And whatever she gave me…' Ianto shook his head. 'I must have lost it in the water. I don't remember how I got back to my flat. I just don't.'

He sat, staring at his reflection in the expensive polished wood. Even now it just seemed wrong.

Gwen was positive, encouraging. 'Well, it was the device that changed you. Maybe her husband's got something that can change you back. If he made it off that boat. If he's alive.'

Ianto looked at the picture of Ross Kielty. Really looked at it. 'He is. I saw him. The other night. He was on St Mary Street. He was shocked to see me.'

'Finally!' Jack grinned. 'We're finally getting somewhere. This is what we do. A bit of CCTV, a bit of digging – and we'll find out where Mr Kielty's gone to ground.'

'But Jack,' said Ianto, 'why did I hear your voice on the boat? And what about those fireballs? Where do they fit in?'

'Oh, we'll deal with them,' said Jack. 'Great balls of fire? It's what I live for.'

JACK IS MAKING A BREAKTHROUGH

Jack stared at the map of Cardiff. 'I'm tracking that energy cloud. There's a spike building up.'

'Really?' said Ianto. 'In what sense?'

Jack scratched the side of his head. 'There's still no overall pattern. But there is one exception. I'd initially discounted it as a blip. But it's been a very constant blip. See this little mini-peak? It's quite separate from the rest of the data. That's still a random cloud of energy fuzz – but this one point, if you track it, over time, is fairly steady. Let's just say, if it was a person, it appears to be mostly around the hotel by the train station.'

'Except late afternoon,' said Ianto, following the chart across the wall.

'When our data peak appears to head across St Mary Street to The Hayes for a cup of tea.'

'I'll go start the SUV,' said Ianto.

THE STRANGE ALIEN DEVICE IS PLOTTING TO TAKE OVER FROM JEREMY KYLE AFTER THIS

Emma pottered around the flat, checking the clock three times a minute. She'd dashed home from work, so many things to do to make herself ready for her date. She'd ignored the voice in her head, assuring her that she'd look amazing and that Rhys would be enormously attracted to her. She just pressed on – sipping on a slightly-too-hot cup-a-soup while she scribbled out a battle list, then managing to shower, do her hair, dry it, style it, do it again, and set it into place while skipping through six different outfits and working out a make-up style somewhere between Marcel Marceau and Jordan.

She suddenly had half an hour to kill. A dead half hour spent prowling round the flat, laughing at articles in *Take A Break,* or flicking through the music channels. She found herself unloading the dishwasher.

The doorbell rang. He was early! All excited she stumbled into her shoes, cursing, and threw open the door. Oh.

'Hi,' said Gwen. 'I'm Gwen.'

'Bloody hell, you're the ex,' hissed Emma, instantly at battle stations.

'Well, er, yes, I suppose so,' she replied, looking mildly annoyed at the admission. As well she might, the cow. 'Look, it's all tricky, but I was wondering if I can pop in for a chat. You know.' A bright little smile.

'A chat? You're actually asking if you can come in, and sit opposite me, sipping on milky instant and talking away in a friendly manner? All girls together, is it?'

'Well, yeah.'

'And then Rhys turns up – and what's he supposed to think of that little picture, eh?'

'Oh, I'll be long gone before that.' Gwen nodded sympathetically.

'Oh, I'm sure you won't be. How's he supposed to move on if you're stalking him, Gwen, luv?'

The big, big smile vanished. 'I'm not here for his benefit. I'm here for yours.' She nudged forward a little.

Emma felt a something build up inside her – like a fire, or a fury, or the biggest sense of disappointment. This was how it always had been, always would be. She'd never get what she wanted. Everything would always fail. Everything would always go wrong. She'd finally meet someone like Rhys and there would be his ex. Ready to trip everything up – always there. Quiet drink in the Bay? Aw, that's great, luv, and Gwen said she'd drop by, isn't that lovely? An evening at the cinema? Let's go see the new Bruce Willis, Gwen said it was dead good. And afterwards we can go to that new Italian place Gwen's been raving about. She'll be there, of course. What a pleasant surprise. Fancy seeing you here.

And suddenly Emma was in the kitchen, watching the kettle boil, finding some cups, spooning coffee into them and making small talk even she wasn't listening to. She noticed limescale was building up around the sink and she thought, 'Oh, I can really have a go at that this weekend,' at some level admitting she wasn't going to have anything better to do.

Somewhere in her head, life and love was about constantly wandering between the bedroom and the living room, about lying next to the man of your dreams in a constant laugh. And yet… Somehow she knew she wouldn't be pottering round the Organic Farmer's Market with Rhys any time soon. And all because of her. Gwen. Who'd clearly just asked her a question. She was sat there, expectantly. A slight pout on her face. A little look of…

'I'm sorry, Gwen. I was miles and miles away.'

I bet you were, thought Gwen. She'd stared round the flat, which was all right in its own way. A bit of her had been praying it was full of empty bottles and cat hair, but it was actually rather neat and a bit stylish. A couple too many scatter cushions, but hey.

Up close, Emma seemed… OK. Gwen had been in the company of killers. Of psychos. Of giant, pure evil. And Emma was none of those things. Emma was just a very pretty woman who didn't seem that sure of herself. 'And what must I seem like?' Gwen thought. 'I must look like the most possessive ex ever.' Which was in some ways a bloody good thing. 'Let her fear me.'

'I said, how did you meet Rhys?'

'Oh,' replied Emma, 'it might sound really silly, but speed-dating. We had an instant connection.'

'Oh, nice,' said Gwen flatly. 'He's told me all about you.'

'Has he?' said Emma. 'He was just so honest and straightforward, you know. So many of the men there… nothing to them. But Rhys – well, I just thought I'd like to see him again.'

'Good,' said Gwen.

'Yes,' said Emma.

There was a second's silence.

'Look, excuse me, but why are you here?' asked Emma, eventually.

'What? Me? Oh, just a friendly chat.'

'It's not normal, though, is it? How long is it since you two split up?'

'Aw, well, ah... couple of months I guess.'

'And you've moved on?'

'Oh, yeah, totally. Yeah. History! Water flushed under the bridge. Whoosh. Still great mates and all, but... Over.'

'It's just that, Gwen, luv, here am I about to go on my first proper date with him, and you turn up.'

'... Yes...'

'That's not normal, is it?'

'Well, we're great mates.'

'Gwen, you should let go.' Emma tilted her head to one side, and reached out a hand to pat her on the arm. 'I don't know what you're trying to do here, but I can tell you how it'll seem to your great mate. He'll think you're sad, lonely and desperate.' She sighed.

Gwen pulled back, puffing up like a bloater fish. 'Hey! It's not like that. It's not like that! If you knew why I was here...'

Emma stood up. 'Oh, Gwen, I know exactly why you're here. There was a time when I was like you. When I was just a bit pathetic. But look at me now. I've moved on up. I've moved on out.'

'And nothing's going to stop you now?' Gwen laughed, despite herself.

Emma smiled. 'Yeah. OK. You got me.' And then her smile froze. 'And you've got a very distinctive laugh.'

'What do you mean by that?' Gwen suddenly sensed danger.

Emma shook her head. 'And I thought I was nuts – but you were there. You were literally at the speed-dating. Along with Rhys. Oh my god – that's so lame. You're actually a stalker. You were there. I remember you at the bar now. Oh, I pity you. Genuinely pity you. And it's been ages since I've pitied anyone.'

'Look,' said Gwen, hotly. 'The truth is—'

Emma didn't listen. She didn't care. She could see something wrong and broken. She could see a world with her and Rhys together – and she could imagine one without Gwen in it. She walked over to the window, quietly reaching for her handbag.

Yes! About bleedin' time, gal!

'Gwen, let me tell you about myself. I was lonely, I wasn't happy. But I kidded myself that everything would be all right. That I didn't have to change myself. That the world would change for me. That I'd find the ideal man without any effort. I was wrong. And I've been blessed with the ability to see all that. To make myself better. To make the world a little better. I've moved on. And I don't have time for people like you any more. You have to understand, Gwen – I've got a picture of an ideal world. And, no matter how lovely you are, you're just not in that picture. Sorry.'

'My god,' thought Gwen, watching as Emma fiddled with her make-up compact. 'This is strange. It's like… megalomania or something. But if she's as dangerous as we thought…'

Oh no, you've got it all wrong.

What?

She doesn't want to rule the world… but I do :)

Gwen stood up, suddenly feeling – her head, oh her legs, that voice, that voice in her head. And Emma standing there, her back to her, laughing. Gwen stretched out a hand horrified to hear the cup falling from her grasp, falling through her arm.

Emma turned around, gave a little gasp and then giggled. Then she saw the mess from the spilt cup, and rushed off to get kitchen roll. She called through, 'Gwen, luv. I've a friend. And this friend understands I don't want you around to ruin my date with Rhys. So we're painting you out of the picture.' She was back, kneeling down and scrubbing at the wet patch of carpet. 'I dunno – perhaps there's a space for you in the world in the end. Perhaps there isn't. But you see, my friend is very powerful – they can change things for the better. For MY better. And I just don't want you around, not at the moment. So let's not have you, eh?'

Gwen tried to run across to her, but only managed a couple of steps. Bringing her face to face with herself in the mirror. Only she wasn't. There was no Gwen in the mirror. Gwen stopped.

Gwen stopped.
And then the doorbell rang.

'Ah, Rhys!'

ROSS KIELTY IS MISTAKEN IN HAPPINESS

'I didn't think…' was all he could say.

The woman opposite him said nothing. She just smiled a little.

He sipped his tea and just looked at her.

'I thought I'd lost you.' He reached out, but she gently batted him away.

'You're not cross, are you?' he asked. 'I know I left you on that boat – but I panicked. There was flame, and horror and I knew they'd come for me. I thought they were after me and that they'd leave you alone and so I ran and never looked back and I knew that that was the right thing and I hoped they'd leave you alone and when you didn't turn up I worried and worried and couldn't reach you and worried some more, but then I see you and I knew I'd done the right thing and do you forgive me? It is all right isn't it, Chris?'

The woman nodded, slowly and sadly.

'I mean, I'm sat here and you come and sit next to me. And we must be all right again, mustn't we? I know it's all so strange at the moment – we had such a good thing going on, and I never dreamt they'd come and do all that. I can tell you, it's been horrible without you to try and sort stuff out. The ferry company are furious.' He laughed and ran a hand through his hair. 'All that paperwork, stuff you wouldn't believe. And so much fuss and the insurance and so on. And the people we were trying to cure – we can't do that now, though. Unless...' A sudden look in his eyes. 'Do you have the machine? We can start again. We can cure more people... we can start over. That is... if you want to.'

She shook her head.

'I didn't think you had it,' he said, sadly. 'But... I still... you know. If you can bear the idea of me, I can very much bear the idea of you. We can do something simpler. When the insurance is all sorted out, we'll have something. Just enough for you and me. I don't think we'll cure the world or anything like we planned – but perhaps we can get just enough for a bit of a life together. A nice little flat in town – not this town, of course, but somewhere nice. You and me and a mortgage. Who'd have thought it when we first met?'

She looked at him, and shrugged.

He babbled on, increasingly sad and desperate. 'All that time ago, and here we are, like a couple of little kids all over again. But they've taken their revenge – perhaps they'll leave us alone now, and we can carry on. Just the two of us. Adam and Eve got cast out of Eden and that must have been a bit of a blow. We've only been cast out of Cardiff. It's not the same. I mean, I'll miss the shopping, but there are some lovely places in Bath. Or Scotland. We could go there. The rain won't be a surprise, and no one will know us there. We've a future there, haven't we? Haven't we, Chris? Oh, Christine... why won't you speak to me?'

'Because I don't know how your wife sounded,' said Ianto.

RHYS IS IN SO MUCH TROUBLE

It had been a long time since Rhys had felt like this. First-date nerves. He'd spent a long time in the shower. Ironed a shirt. Worried in case people still wore ties ('No, no one still wears ties'), even rifled the dusty bathroom cabinet and found some breath-fresh spray. It'd been fun dancing round the flat to some good old Oasis while getting dressed – like going out on the lash a decade ago. All aggro and after-sport deodorant.

He stopped to look at himself in the hall mirror, and had to admit, 'Looking good, mate.' He walked over to Emma's with a spring in his step. And, oddly, he didn't think of Gwen at any point. Not when showering, not when trying to find matching socks (a job that normally required two cries for help). Not when walking over, not when stopping to buy a little bunch of flowers (tacky, but spur of the moment, and they were lovely blooms that smelt of freshness and excitement).

He looked round at Emma's street and thought how she had such a nice little house on a street that was... definitely up and coming. He noticed how many places there were along the way to have a good fry-up, and he thought, 'Well, that's nice,' and found himself looking forward to the morning.

He'd had a great day. He'd loved the way that people had quietly noticed how good he was looking at the moment. It made him feel great. It made him feel wonderful. He'd spent the whole day looking forward to this moment – to seeing Emma again, and making her happy. He hoped he could make her happy.

He buzzed and, after a few seconds, the door to her flat sprung open, and they smiled at each other. She looked even better than he remembered. There was something about her that said 'home'. Something that said comfort and welcome and the best bits of childhood. But also something about her that said wildness and fun and watching the sun come up.

'Ah, Rhys!' she said.

He kissed her. Just slightly on the lips. And he loved how she smelled.

'It's good to see you,' she said, and he glowed. 'You're just in time. Come in for a moment. We'll have a glass of wine before we go out, shall we?'

And he noticed that she was carrying some kitchen roll and cleaning up, and he relaxed even more. She was human – she cleaned. She was perfection.

He noticed a slight burning smell too, and sniffed the air. She giggled. 'Oh that must be the bread-maker. I've always got a loaf on, you know.'

And Rhys smiled even more. She took away the flowers, with much praise, and placed them in a vase on the coffee table. And Rhys didn't even notice that she was tidying away two empty coffee cups. He just thought how right his flowers looked on her coffee table.

He settled back onto the sofa, and he was pleased that she sat down next to him, draping an arm around him. 'Tonight's going to be lovely, isn't it?' she said, kissing him gently on the cheek.

'Oh, I hope so,' he said honestly. 'I'd hate to disappoint you. I can honestly say that you're one of the most wonderful women I've ever met. And this is gorgeous wine.'

'Thank you,' she said, clinking their glasses with a laugh. 'And it goes perfectly with your lovely eyes.'

'Oh, my eyes, is it?' said Rhys. 'Is that all you like about me?'

Rhys put down his glass on the coffee table, pleased that she hadn't even asked him to use a coaster. And he just looked at her. And then they kissed again, properly.

JACK IS SOFTLY, SOFTLY CATCHEE MONKEY

People came and went across The Hayes. It was the centre of old Cardiff, in some ways. Known as the Hayes Island, a little cobbled area surrounded by department stores and endless building works. In the middle of the Island was a snack bar, pumping out hot, sweet tea and bacon rolls and hot cross buns and cakes to people who were happy to sit in the wintry open air, shivering and blowing on their drinks and passing the time.

It was quiet today. A few lonely old couples sat comparing bargains found and lost. A comical Frenchman from Poland stood, trying to sell onions from the back of an old black bicycle. A tired-looking kid was handing out flyers about God.

Jack sipped his drink and watched the figures two tables away. There was Ianto, and there was Ross Kielty. They looked quiet. There'd been an initial blow-up and he'd thought about crossing over and interceding, but Ianto just averted it, laying a gentle hand on the man's shoulder. And he'd fallen forward, crying. And Ianto had hugged him. And then they'd spoken for a bit. And now they were running out of things to say. And the man was crying again. Jack realised his drink had gone cold. He went over to the counter and asked for three more. And a Bakewell slice. He took them over to the table and sat down.

Ross sniffed miserably and looked up. 'Who's this?'

Ianto smiled. 'This is my boss, Jack.'

'Your boss?'

Jack shook his hand, Ross returning it without much enthusiasm. 'Ianto is my Man Friday. Even at the moment. He keeps me honest and good.'

Ianto sipped his tea. Hot and milky and sweet. He noticed he was leaving a lipstick mark on the cardboard cup and thought, 'I'm never going to get used to this, am I?'

Jack continued. 'He was on that ferry because of me. I'm responsible for what's happened to him. But I could, so easily, make you responsible. For all of it – for the deaths, the destruction, for what's going on in Cardiff, even now. But really, that's just routine. What I really want is to know what happened to Ianto, and how I get him back.'

Ianto smiled, and reached over, snapping off a chunk of Bakewell.

Jack gave him a glance. 'You'll put on weight.'

Ross laughed. 'Christine used to think so, too. But no – the body's perfect. It doesn't really gain that much weight. It just stays fairly lean and trim and fresh. It doesn't really age. I should know – since she's been gone, I've been lost. I've been pushing this body to the limits – and every day it snaps back to how it was.'

'Dorian Gray,' mused Jack.

'If you like – but there's no painting in the attic.'

'Oh there is,' said Jack grimly. 'There's always a picture in the attic. There's always a bill to be paid. What did you do? What happened?'

'Well,' said Ross. 'We were designers and decorators. You know how it is. We made a lot of money. We made each other very happy. And we had these clients – and they were like friends. And they were the most beautiful couple. I mean, gay, so obviously, looked after themselves, and what have you, but they were really, really wonderful. Great to work for, and somehow you knew just what it was they wanted. It was the easiest job we'd ever worked on. And we could just wander in and out of the flat and they didn't mind. They were very free and easy and we felt... we were their best friends. Although they had a lot of best friends. Some would be around for a few weeks, some for just one night. But we were there for a while – we had work to do. We had decorating to do. And we felt fulfilled, worthwhile. We were making somewhere suitable for them.

'And one day, they were out, or in bed or something. And there was this tiny ornament. Christine found it first. She just noticed it on a shelf. She said it was calling out to her. She said it was all forgotten and lonely and it wanted to be taken away. And she said we should do that. And we did.

'And it told us what to do. Honestly. As soon as we both touched it, it was there in our heads. Christine said it sounded like her dad. For me, it sounded just like Richard bloody Burton. But somehow, that object talked to us. Soothing and strong and lovely.

'And we left the flat, and we never looked back. It made us beautiful. Oh, we were great before – but it made everything we ever worried about go away. And after it had done that, it asked us if there was anything more we wanted. World Peace, Chris said. It laughed, but I said it would be nice to do something good. And the little stone said that that could be arranged.

'Took a couple of months, mind. Keeping underground, realising that we could use the ferry service as a cover. Letting word of mouth spread subtly. We lived in Dublin, only took the journey once a week. Kept a low profile. We weren't sure what we'd done, but we figured it wasn't best to make a noise. And then... well, the newspaper thing came out, and for some reason I knew we'd gone a step too far. I don't know if it was the picture with Christine in it, or the cheek that I'd let myself get quoted. But we looked at it, and we worried. But we figured we were doing good. We were making a lot of money, yeah, but we were really making a difference. Certainly a lot more than decorating. You know how it is.'

They all nodded.

'And then… then it all happened. And I'm sorry – I'm sorry for you, and for all those people – and for Christine. But I dunno. Were we doing the right thing? I'll always think we were, but I don't know. I've just been sat in Cardiff, waiting for someone to find me, really. To tell me.'

'OK,' said Jack.

'And?' Ross looked up, his beautiful face somehow tired and stretched and marked. 'Did I do the right thing?'

Jack shrugged. 'We feel how we think. There's a bigger picture here – and it depends how much of it you want to see. On every flea another flea feeds. And what suck'd you first suck'd me. John Donne, maybe. Do you know what will happen to Ianto? Can you cure him?'

Ross shook his head. 'Only the device can do that. Maybe. You really don't have it?' He looked suddenly hopeful.

Ianto smiled. 'No. And I don't think we would give it to you if we had it.'

'It's a toy of the gods,' said Jack, his face hardening. 'Wouldn't you say?'

Ross looked terribly sad.

Jack scraped his chair back and stood up. 'Come on, Ianto, we have work to do. Thank you for your time. We shan't meet again, Mr Kielty. Make the most of your life.'

He strode away.

Ianto turned and shrugged, the movement suddenly all wrong in the body. 'I'm sorry for your loss,' he said, and walked off into the rain.

Ross watched the figure of his wife walk down the road, turn a corner, and vanish for ever.

IANTO IS EXPLAINING HOW COFFEE IS LIKE LIFE

They didn't talk on the way back to the Hub, though Jack was swearing at each and every traffic light. They parked, and Jack strode ahead, his coat billowing in the rain.

Ianto followed behind, limping slightly and cursing his choice of shoes – strange little heels that scooped in the rain and soaked his toes and the skirt just felt wrong, and the pants had shifted, attacking his bum like cheesewire and... Oh, never mind.

They walked down the fire escape without talking, and Jack stomped into Torchwood. He marched up to his map of the energy cloud, and groaned. Then he threw his coat down and slumped across a sofa.

Ianto hovered, felt ridiculous, and pottered through into his area, where he started to bang about. 'The secret is not to burn the beans. Well, scald, really. Coffee scalds at 98 degrees. A lot of baristas insist on 100 degrees when they make their coffee – lots of steam and effect, but you ruin the flavour. That's why it tastes like it's made from old batteries – and that's why you drown it in milk and ginger and cream and foam and chocolate sprinkles – there's something wrong with the fundamental ingredient, and rather than admit it, you press on, you dress it up, you disguise it. You don't talk about the problem, you wrap it up in sugar and glitter. Isn't that right?'

He handed Jack a cup, who took it automatically. Didn't say anything, not even thanks.

Ianto sat down on the sofa next to him, legs not quite in the right order, sipping carefully at his own cup and waiting.

He waited for a full two minutes before Jack looked him in the eye. And then Jack smiled, and cuffed him gently on the ear. 'Oh, Ianto Jones,' he said, and stopped.

'What's wrong? Are we going to talk about it?'

Jack sipped the coffee.

'Oh, Ianto. Owen and Gwen and Suzie and Tosh and you – you all spend so much time telling me that the world isn't simple, that not all aliens are evil, that it's worth working out why people are here – that I shouldn't be the ruthless dark one. And sometimes you're right. And sometimes you're wrong. All this is my fault. All this is because I made an agreement. An arrangement.'

He sipped the coffee again and gave Ianto a look that made him feel very frightened.

GWEN IS NOWHERE, AND IT'S FOR BLOODY EVER

Around her, the old house creaked and yawned, timber cracking like a weary boat at sea. And she just stood there, feet planted solidly on the off-cream carpet, frozen in time just between the sofa and the coffee table.

Time moved oddly around her, and she recognised the pull in the air of Rift Energy. Which started to explain things. Emma's little device had reached out and trapped her just outside now. And she wasn't alone. She could sense other figures, distantly, as though across a vast space. She tried shouting but couldn't – if she squinted she could somehow perceive about a dozen female figures stood-stock still a long way away... all of them done up to the nines and dressed to kill. She realised she was glimpsing the missing women from speed-dating. They were still there in Tombola's. She wondered how they were coping after several days outside of time.

It was a place that was, to be frank, boring and very itchy. She was burning with the desire to scratch her left leg. Left leg first, and then definitely right bum cheek, upper back and then her nose. Plus behind both ears. Urgggh.

Her feet ached. She wondered how much worse that would get. And how much more tired she would get. She ached, she felt tired. She wanted to curl up and sleep. But she couldn't really move. And all around her was the world of Emma's flat – eternity spread out across the lounge and towards the kitchenette.

And blocking the view of the universe were Rhys and Emma kissing. They were getting ready to go out, and there was nothing she could do to stop them. She screamed herself hoarse, yelling out Rhys's name with rage and fear and panic and fury. But no. Nothing.

Emma kissed Rhys on the cheek. 'And where are you taking me? Is it somewhere wonderful? It had better be.'

Rhys leant close. 'Oh yes. Best view of the Bay, it is. Just you and me.'

'I can't wait.' Emma giggled. 'Oh, you're wonderful.' She kissed him again on the cheek and picked up her handbag.

Rhys held the door open for her and Emma sailed through, glancing over her shoulder to smirk at Gwen.

And then they were gone. And just Gwen, trapped and alone and motionless in this bloody terrible little flat, itch itch itch, and oh god, she's left the radio tuned to *Classic*.

CAPTAIN JACK, CAPTAIN JACK, GET OFF YOUR BACK, GO INTO TOWN, DON'T LET US DOWN. OH NO, NO.

Jack was waiting impassively for the invisible lift when Ianto caught up with him.

'I have to go. Don't follow me, Ianto. This is all my fault.' Jack was grim.

'What do you mean?'

'I made a mistake,' said Jack. 'I caused all this. I'll either be back in an hour, or not at all.' He shrugged. 'But hey – you know me. I'm tough.'

'Don't be bloody rubbish.'

Jack stepped onto the platform, which started its upward glide. Rain was pouring down around him.

Straining to see him, Ianto tried to jump up on tiptoe and felt foolish.

'You can't just go!' he protested, amazed at how high his voice went. 'You can't just run off like this!'

He could just see Jack, staring back down, giving him a look. It was a look that didn't belong with the smile that forced its way across his face.

'Jack!' screamed Ianto as Jack started to vanish through the ceiling.

He just caught Jack's voice, floating back down to him.

'Check the energy cloud, Ianto. It's building up – and there's about a day before it goes off the scale.' And then he was gone.

MOZART IS SPONSORED BY CHOLESTRIA

… now available in a delicious dairy-free drink.

Next up on I Spy a Maestro… I Spy someone beginning with B. Would anyone care to guess? Don't forget, we've just had P for lovely Pachelbel, and M was for magnificent Mozart, dear Wolfgang Amadeus – but B. Well, there's almost two choices there. Shall I play you a mystery track and then we'll take your calls on the usual number? So sit back, relax, and pop your thinking caps on…

Gwen was bored and scared. Like waiting for test results. This was boredom with a creeping numbness. The itching had gone now. And all she had was this vague lack of sensation. And on top of the tedium, a creeping, creeping loss of… she felt tired, could almost sense her eyes closing, and knew that this could mean a sleep that she'd never wake up from. The minutes crept gently into hours. Her only hope was that perhaps nothing dreadful was happening, that perhaps Rhys would be all right (oh, please let him be all right) and that maybe Emma would come back alone, and she'd see sense and release her. Oh, if Rhys was all right and she could get out then she'd be fine about it. Honest she would.

… Don't forget, you'll need to be licensed to sponsor an immigrant!

And welcome back to three hours of the most slinky and relaxing music imaginable.

The key turned in the lock and Emma and Rhys fell through in a laughing, snogging heap, dragging and fumbling their way onto the couch. Gwen was gutted.

For a second she hoped that her rage and fear might let her do something. Might let her move, or that he'd hear her. That he'd stop. That he'd realise… She struggled and struggled. But she couldn't move. And she just watched.

Every now and then, Emma shot a glance of triumph in Gwen's direction. Gwen wanted to scream back. Emma had taken her life, and she was now taking Rhys – Rhys who wasn't Rhys, Rhys who she'd changed, who she was somehow making do… this…

'And you're making me watch. When I get out of here, I am going to hurt you.'

Emma stood up, zipping down her top and throwing back her hair. 'Oh, you're a wild one, Rhys Williams. No wonder your ex couldn't let you go.'

Rhys spluttered on his wine. 'My ex? Not Gwen?'

'Oh yes!' said Emma brightly. 'I met her in the street. She warned me away from you. Said you were bad news. I told her she was pathetic and that you'd moved on.'

'Ohhhhh, good,' said Rhys uncertainly, suddenly rather more like himself. He looked nervously round the room. 'You did, did you?'

Gwen was roaring away invisibly. 'Yes! Rhys! Yes! Come on, baby! Think. Remember me – you've got to remember me!'

'Oh yeah,' said Emma, with the faint air of a schoolgirl telling a really big fib. 'I told her a few home truths. You were too good for her, and she knew it.'

Rhys looked around the room again, and glanced sickly

back at her. 'You told her this, did you?' He glanced over at the window, as though expecting Gwen to come crashing through it with a machine gun.

Emma nodded. 'Trust me. She's history. I laid it down to her and she just had to take it. The truth hurts, but it works. You. Will. Never. See. Her. Again.' And she laughed and reached out her hand, glancing over at Gwen. And Rhys took her hand, at first gently, and then placidly, a dopey grin spreading across his face.

Gwen suddenly knew that she'd lost him. That Rhys was gone, replaced with the plastic sheep. She howled. Howled with rage and frustration. She was dying, and Rhys was lost – Emma would use him, change him, and then when she got bored, he'd die too. Just like that. And there was nothing she could do but watch. Watch and rage. She never dreamt this would be the end – watching everything taken away from her so cruelly and slowly.

Rhys stood up, gathering Emma in his arms. She leaned into his ear and breathed, 'Take me to bed, Rhys.'

'Don't go, Rhys. Please don't go. I love you, Rhys!'

Rhys followed her to the door. And paused.

'Er, why is Gwen's bag by your sofa?'

'Yes! Oh, Rhys, you beauty! I love you! Yes!'

Emma's gaze fell on the bag, and froze, and then she glanced across at where Gwen was.

Gwen felt a flicker of joy, of hope.

For the first time, Emma looked desperate, human. She could

see the thinking going on. 'God, how did you get in this mess?' Gwen thought.

'Oh, Rhys!' gasped Emma after slightly too long a pause. 'Gwen's bag? Oh my god! Has she broken in? Is she trying to scare us? Oh, Rhys, call the police!' She clung to him.

Rhys reacted as he always did when faced with tears, curling up with embarrassment – but in this case, also suspicion. 'Gwen's... Oh, my love, are you sure she didn't come here, talk to you? Leave it behind by mistake?'

'No,' Emma sniffed, quietly.

He detached himself, and picked up the handbag. He looked inside it, almost automatically. And then he put it down, quietly.

'I love Gwen,' he said. 'She's my wife.'

'What?' Emma looked up, sudden real grief slapped on her face. 'No, no. You love me.'

Rhys shook his head. 'I'm sorry. No. I remember her now. She's my wife and I love her. Where is she, please?' His voice had gone tough.

Emma ignored him, rifling instead in her own handbag. 'No, no, no,' she said flatly. 'You love me, now. You love me!'

She was suddenly holding the little glowing pebble in her hands, turning it over and over.

Do it girl! Do it!

'Oh god, Rhys!'

Gwen started to scream his name over and over as Emma turned to face him.

'What's that?' asked Rhys as she held it sheepishly towards him.

'It's a gun! It's a bloody space gun and she's pointing it at you!

Oh, Rhys, oh, she's going to change you again.'

Emma paused. It was the careful, slow pause of a shy child showing you her favourite toy. On the one hand, she was proud of it and wanted you to know what it meant to her. On the other hand it was so precious, she didn't really want to give it up to you. So she'd offer it out with a firm grip and eyes pregnant with tears.

'I don't know exactly...' began Emma. 'But it makes everything special. Would you like to see how it works?' And she stretched out with it, almost like she was offering it.

But Gwen knew better, Gwen knew what was going to happen next. Oh, Rhys...

And suddenly Rhys lunged at her, plucking it out of Emma's shaking grasp.

'Where did you...?' he began, and then he stopped. His face slowed down, and took on the surprised, worried expression that Gwen got to see whenever she asked him if he'd paid the water bill.

And something in Emma changed. She looked startled, and then lost. Desperate. 'Where've you gone, Cheryl?' she said, quietly.

Rhys didn't hear her. But Gwen did.

Gwen woke up, lying on the sofa. Rhys was kneeling over her, concerned. When she saw him she laughed and hugged him, delighted to be able to smell his smell and actually hold him.

'Where's she gone? Where's she gone?' Gwen yelled, but he shushed her.

'Relax,' he said, beaming. 'Just so happens, I'm deputy manager of the Department of Saving Your Arse. Emma is... not a problem.' He jerked his head over his shoulder.

Gwen sat up, and looked.

Standing there like a cross, mildly overweight waxwork with bad skin and terrible hair, was Emma. Not moving, not capable of moving, but fading away, ever so slightly.

Gwen giggled and then stopped herself. 'Oh my god. What have you done? Rhys?'

Rhys looked abashed. 'It was the voice in my head, see. Told me it was either you or her. No contest, really.'

Gwen got up with difficulty and walked over to Emma. And sighed.

She turned around. 'Voice in your head, Rhys Williams? Is this like the one that told you to buy 150 tickets on Rollover week?'

'No.' He held up the pebble, which glowed and glistened. 'This is one of your Extra Terrestrial Artefacts, isn't it?' He shook it, proudly, and winced. 'Ouch. Apparently, I'm not supposed to do that.'

Gwen held out her hand. 'Give that here, Rhys.'

Rhys didn't. 'If it's all the same to you, love, I won't just now. I've only just got you back, and I'm not letting go until I'm certain that it's a permanent state of affairs, so to speak.'

'I see.' Gwen wasn't fooled. 'You like having a voice in your head, don't you?'

Caught out, Rhys gave her a guilty look. 'I *really* like having a voice in my head. It's dead good. At first it sounded just like Arnie, but now it's doing a pretty good David Beckham. All squeaky and puzzled. It's really sweet. Especially when it just explained temporal causality to me.'

Gwen prodded Emma. 'And what happens to her?'

Rhys shrugged. 'Nothing for the moment. She just stays frozen. The device says Jack will know what to do.'

'Jack?' said Gwen, troubled.

'But, if you ask me, it's for the best, you know. I've met women like her. Never happy with other people, never happy with herself. Trust me, nothing and no one's ever good enough for her. She was using the machine to find the right man – and there's no such thing as Mr Perfect.'

Gwen hugged him again. 'No there isn't – but we do our best, don't we?'

'Yeah,' said Rhys. 'I know what all your faults are, and you tell me what all mine are.'

'Quite right. Shall we go home?'

'Oh yes.'

Gwen opened the door for him and pecked him on the cheek. 'Thank you,' she said. 'I don't know what I'd have done without you.'

'Thanks, pet.'

'Even if you did kiss another woman in front of me.'

Rhys protested. 'But I was her love slave! I was helpless in the face of her desires.'

'Doesn't matter. It's still all your fault. And, on the journey home, I'll explain how.'

'Oh lovely.'

'Come on,' Gwen paused in the doorway, desperately happy. 'Oh, and let's leave her the radio on, shall we?'

YVONNE IS NOW LIVING IN A FISH RESTAURANT

It was early morning when Gwen made it to the Hub.

When they'd got back to the flat, she'd just wanted to crawl into bed, but she'd made herself turn right around and head back out. Well, almost.

She'd tried phoning, but no one had answered her. When she arrived, the cavernous office was silent.

She suddenly realised how empty the enormous place was. How quiet and cold. A gentle ticking came from the Rift Manipulator.

'Hello?' she cried.

She went over to the coffee machine and felt it. Stone cold.

This was a bad sign.

No Jack. No Ianto.

A sudden horrible thought struck her – what if they'd died? Would that make her Torchwood? Would she be the last line of defence for Cardiff, Wales and occasionally Earth?

Bums.

There was a noise behind her, and with relief she saw Ianto climbing out of an accessway. He was looking... amazing. Grubby, but amazing. He was in a long Fifties-retro dress with a work smock wrapped around it. His hair was hidden under a scarf. He was covered in dust and a couple of scratch marks. He smiled and shook out a duster.

'Hey, Gwen!' he said a little too brightly. 'How are you?'

'Oh, amazing. Where've you been?'

'Small vermin problem. Well, large vermin problem really. The Rift's causing minor mutations to nearby wildlife. Luckily the rats aren't getting bigger – just longer tails, but the shrews are enormous. And have started singing.'

'You should get a cat,' said Gwen.

Ianto looked a bit sad. 'Oh, they had a cat before I joined. Yvonne. But no one's seen her since we got the pterodactyl.'

'Oh.'

He shrugged, a little sadly. 'Oh I'm sure she's fine – Yvonne was very cunning, by all accounts. But Jack had me going through the pterodactyl's stools for a month looking for evidence.'

Gwen grimaced. 'Where is the Fearless Leader?'

Ianto was again a bit too bright. 'Oh, I'm sure he's around.'

'Have you tried calling him?'

'Yes,' admitted Ianto.

'And he's not answering you?'

'No.'

'Ah.'

'I'm sure he'll turn up.' Ianto sank miserably down onto the sofa and cradled his chin in his hands.

'You've said that already.'

'Not quite that, I think you'll find. I used a broadly similar but equally evasive turn of phrase.'

'But Ianto, this is important, Rhys and I have solved the speed-dating thing.'

'That's great, Gwen, really great,' said Ianto, flatly.

'Hey! What's up?' said Gwen, losing it a little. 'This is big news. We brought back a talking pebble and everything.'

She pulled the evidence bag gently out of her jacket.

Ianto started with horror and surprise. 'That... that's the thing that... I found on the boat. Before I changed.'

Both of them had a few seconds of just breathing very, very hard. And staring at the device, glowing gently through the bonded polythene-carbide bag.

'Well, bugger me,' said Gwen, eventually.

Ianto's voice was soft, and scared. Gwen noticed he was chewing the end of his hair. 'The energy cloud, this object. Jack said it was all his fault somehow. He said he knew who was behind it. And he went off to find them.'

'Oh, that's brilliant!'

'Not really – he went off nearly twelve hours ago. I've tried everything to find him, and I can't. He's vanished.'

Gwen suddenly understood Ianto's mood. She put the device down on the desk and frowned. 'I can see why you're worried. I mean, what could Jack have been doing all night?'

THE PERFECTION ARE RUTHLESS, TIRELESS AND HAVE A HIGH THREAD COUNT

And, on the other side of Cardiff, Jack Harkness fell back exhausted on the bed and cried out, 'Please fellas, not again!'

3. DAMAGED GODS

GOD IS DEAD (BORED)

The city was made of silver and glass and spun and twisted across the surface of the planet like a brilliant thread.

Wherever the sun struck it, it glowed, the metal singing with heat and light and brilliance. Everywhere there was a song in the air, and a warmth.

It was, visitors had said, like the first day of spring, but forever.

Outside the city, grass of the greenest hue washed down towards a beach whose sand was, to some eyes, just a little pink.

And up and down crawled creatures – such creatures, like insects carved from jewels, or jewels grown out of insects. And each creature, as it moved, made a little noise with its wings – a happy little sound of wonder and joy. If the creatures flew, it was to make merry little trips up to the very highest tower, where they hung happily for a few seconds before drifting gently away on a warm breeze to settle somewhere else.

And inside the spire, at the top of a thousand beautiful steps that the insects would occasionally crawl dutifully up, in a hall made of glass polished by the sun of a thousand years, sat two beings. They were content. They had been content for centuries, and would be content for centuries more.

Everything was perfect.

But there was a third being in the room. And the third being was actually terribly bored.

JACK IS REMEMBERING AN AGREEMENT

Three years ago…

Jack stepped into the club. Cigarette smoke hung heavy in the air; there was a pounding fanfare from the quiz machine. Behind the bar was a formidable array of house spirits, tapped beers, alcopops and crisps. Above it was a chalked sign – 'We can cater for your civil partnership' – next to a faded warning about drugs.

By the bar was a little DJ booth, in which a starveling Emo kid stood, mixing tracks unhappily in only a pair of jockeys and some boots. Jack sighed.

He looked around the room – the barman/woman (Jack couldn't really tell) had already tensed and was trying to out-pout him. There were three drunk old men laughing at each other's jokes. There was a lesbian couple rowing tiredly at a table over a packet of peanuts – one had her arm in plaster, the other was on crutches. A lone businessman sat leafing through a copy of the *Pink Paper* that was sodden with spilt beer. On the dance floor, a man in a backwards baseball cap was trying to do, dear god, the Running Man.

And then there was…

Well, hullo, boys!

Jack got himself a glass of water and made his way over.

'Do you mind if I join you?'

'Not at all. We wondered when you'd make an appearance.'

Jack sat down at the stool and looked at the two men. He smiled, impressed despite himself.

'Is it your first human form, fellas? If so, I have to say, pretty good.'

One of the couple shrugged. They were, Jack thought, amazing. Just over six foot, mid twenties, clear blue eyes – one blond and preppy, the other dark-haired and olive-skinned. Simple, fitted T-shirts, expensive jeans – neither garment concealing any of the muscle that was rippling underneath. Both were staring at him, quiet amusement dancing across their deep blue eyes. 'I can just imagine them advertising underwear,' thought Jack. And then he dwelt on the thought a little too long. He realised he was supposed to say something.

'You guys are a dream. I'm impressed.'

The dark one spread his hands out modestly. 'Oh – consider us a work in progress. We want to be perfect.'

Jack smiled even more. 'I see.'

'You want to ask us some questions, don't you?' The blond seemed mildly amused. 'I take it you are Torchwood.'

'Yes, I am. And if you know us, you know that I'm not here to ask you questions. We protect the Earth from alien threats.'

'And is that what we are? Alien threats? Puh-lease. I'm just Brendan,' said the blond.

'And I'm Jon,' the dark-haired one shook Jack's hand. It was a firm, warm handshake, and Jack grinned into Jon's eyes despite himself.

'Nice,' he said. 'Nice manners, guys. Very charming. So when does the killing start?'

Both of them laughed. Laughed like Jack was a toddler who'd said something funny.

'There'll be none of that. That's not in our nature.'

'Then what are you?'

'We're the Perfection.'

Jack grinned again. 'Smug aliens. Great. What does the name mean?'

'The Perfection are gods, Jack.' Brendan's tone was gentle.

'Is that so?' Jack took a long drink of his water, and suddenly wished for something stronger. 'I've met quite a few gods. Most of them were just conmen with great gadgets.'

Brendan smiled sweetly. 'I hear your argument. But we are the Perfection.' It wasn't an answer. 'We are very old gods, Jack. We've spread a slow arc of perfection across the universe. We stay for millennia, we make everything perfect. And then, eventually, when all is wonderful, we move on.'

'Leaving a dustbowl in your wake.'

Jon shook his head. 'Not at all. When a society is functioning as well as is possible – then our work is done. When a people no longer need their gods, we must bow and leave the stage.'

'No doubt to rapturous applause.'

Brendan laid a hand softly on Jack's. 'Underneath that cynicism, you're hoping that we're real. Let yourself trust us, Jack. Hallam's World, the Province of Sovertial, the Min Barrier – these are but the latest in our projects. Worlds known across the galaxy for their harmony, stability and peace. Not, perhaps, utopia, but the very best they can be.'

Jack nodded, impressed. Hallam's World – he'd once been stationed at the Time Agency outpost there. The most boring time of his life. Everything was like a warm Sunday afternoon just after lunch and before the television got good. But... in their own way, decent people. Very good people.

Jon smiled. 'You yourself are an outsider – born on another world, making the most of this one. And that's all we want to do.'

Jack sneered. 'I see. And in six months – what? A brave new Reich of joy and harmony?'

'Oh god, no!' chuckled Brendan, lighting a fag. Jack blinked.

'I said we are old gods. We've spent millennia building worlds where the skies burned with thought and our names were written in gold across the moons. Pfft!' he exhaled wearily.

'We're knackered,' sighed Jon. 'It's all such… work. We just wanted something a little smaller.'

'Wales?' offered Jack, mulling it over. The PM would be pissed, but…

'No. Not even Cardiff. The Welsh are such a strong people – and, frankly, much prefer talking to God than listening. No. Look around you.'

Jack looked around the bar.

'What?'

'This. This tiny little group of disparate little outcasts. This gay community. Oh, they could be so beautiful, so fabulous, couldn't they? But it's all so drab and tired and joyless. Why – look at the hair, Jack. This is a gay scene where the mullet never went out. Couldn't it all be more fun?'

Jack sat there. Sipping his water. And thinking.

'No, hang on,' he said.

Sip. Think.

'Let me just check.'

Sip. Think.

Actually, when was this glass last cleaned?

'So, you just want to give the gay scene a makeover?'

Brendan and Jon nodded together.

'And it's not going to involve some weird ritual sacrifice?'

Jon shook his head vehemently. 'Oh lordy, no. How old school are you, sweet cheeks? We'll just lead by example. It's how we work. We are the Perfection. There's no magic – wherever we go, people adore us, they love us, they want to be more like us. And we help them. But we don't cheat. We don't steal. We just bask in their love and we grow stronger. That's all we want – to be wanted.'

Jack grinned at them with disbelief.

'I really still think you could be evil. This could all be a horrible, horrible thing. It would be easier to just drag you down to the cells. Job done.'

Jon shuddered, theatrically, and laid his hand on Jack's arm, muscles incidentally tensing magnificently, like weasels in a sack. 'It would be easier, yes, but not as much fun.'

Brendan stubbed out his cigarette and grinned. 'And you won't. You trust us. You like us. You'll give us a chance. And you'll stay for another drink. A proper drink.'

Jack gazed sadly at his glass. 'I'd love to, but I have to be ready. For when everything changes.'

Jon turned back from the bar, three drinks in his hand. 'Trust us – you'll be fine for a few hours. God's word.'

A few minutes later…

'Brendan,' said Jack. 'Your boyfriend's hand is on my leg.'

'Oh,' said Brendan. 'Is that a problem?'

Jack grinned. 'Not at all. I just wondered if you felt left out.'

Brendan shrugged. 'Not really.' And placed his hand on Jack's other leg.

'Ah, I see. Does anyone ever say no to you guys?'

Jon tipped his head on one side, puzzled. 'Why would they? We're perfect!'

And the Perfection laughed, together. Not at all creepily.

And, about an hour later…

'OK,' muttered Jack happily into the pillow. 'I'm open to making a deal.'

Somewhere, Brendan gave a muffled laugh. 'Oh, you're open to a lot more than that.'

'Yup,' admitted Jack, giggling.

Jon leaned in close, his voice joining the blissful throbbing in Jack's head. 'You're prepared to consider an arrangement?'

'Yeah. I just wish more people tried your approach. So much

more fun than waving around weapons.'

'Really?' Jon kissed Jack. The kiss was perfect. 'But you're such a skilled diplomat. And we don't have any guns.'

Jack felt Jon move away from him, and started to laugh. 'Hey guys. Don't think I'm not extraordinarily grateful.' He smiled, dreamily, and just enjoyed himself for a while. 'I hate to ruin the moment, but just a reminder. It ain't gonna stop me having a good time, but if you let me down, I won't hesitate in coming back here guns blazing.'

Brendan laughed, pleasantly, and moved up the bed to wrap his arms around Jack's shoulders. 'How evil would we have to be just to get you to come back?'

Jack beamed. 'Oh, barely evil at all. Just a little naughty. But remember – you start hurting people, and, charming as you are, fun as this is, and .... absolutely great as that is, Jon – it's not gonna stop me blowing you away.'

Jon laughed.

Jack smirked. 'Howabout, I love it when a plan comes together?'

A year later…

Jack bumped into them at Cardiff Gay Pride. He was covered in mud and a scrap of blood-spattered gingham.

Brendan and Jon stood underneath a gold umbrella, watching the downpour. They were just wearing tight jeans and body paint. They waved to him.

'Hey, guys,' said Jack. 'I'd love to stop and chat, but… you know… alien menace.'

'Grr!' they both mimed claws.

'Yeah. Exactly. Lots of tentacles, big gun, gingham dress. Seen it?'

They shook their heads.

'So, how are you?' asked Brendan.

Jack shrugged. 'Keepin' busy. Saving the world. You?'

'So-so,' said Jon. 'Look around you – we've already improved the hair.'

'That was you?' laughed Jack. 'Way to go, guys.'

'The last mullet moved to Swansea the other week. We had a party. Lasted a few days.'

'Few other things – you know. Stern words with innocent boys down from Treorchy for the weekend. You know – always use a jonny, and no, a Mars Bar wrapper's not a substitute. The STD clinic's dead chuffed. Talked about giving us a plaque, which was sweet. Plus, by just being ourselves, I think we've been a good influence.'

'Yeah,' said Brendan. 'People have finally stopped wearing plaid. And I'm doing some great work with the Assembly.'

'I'm impressed,' said Jack.

'Care to show us?' asked Brendan, raising an eyebrow. If anything they'd got prettier. Something even more striking about his cheekbones. And. Oh. Monster. Right.

Jack looked over, reluctantly, to the main stage. He could hear roaring and a few screams. 'I'd love to. Maybe later?'

Brendan and Jon followed his glance to where Cardiff's queen of song stood, drenched as usual, belting out 'Delilah' over a sodden PA. There was a flash of gingham and a tentacle backstage. Over the rain, Jack could just hear the sound of automatic gunfire. As he watched, Owen backed onto the stage, desperately aiming a flamethrower into the wings. He became gradually aware of the crowd, and grinned sheepishly, dropping into the kind of guilty creep that he'd seen roadies use. He paused and winked at the singer, who somehow carried on singing despite Owen aiming a jet of flame into the lighting rig. A large, charred tentacle flopped onto the stage next to them, and lay there, flailing and smoking.

Jon applauded, ironically. 'That boy's got to be one of yours,' he smirked. 'Torchwood are never throwing me a surprise birthday.'

Brendan leaned in and kissed Jack quickly. 'Go!' he urged. 'Save Charlotte Church. We'll be around tonight. We're having a White Party.'

Jack saluted and ran off.

And two years later, Jack found himself back at the club where it all began…

CAPTAIN JACK HAS KILLED THE WABBIT, KILLED THE WABBIT

Jack made his way slowly across the dance floor. Partly because it was packed. Partly because it was packed with strikingly attractive, topless men. On the one hand, he wore a look of grim determination. On the other, it seemed like a good party.

A particularly muscled guy with a big grin wrapped himself around Jack and started to dance against him slowly. He drew himself close to Jack, and Jack leaned slowly in and whispered quietly in his ear. 'Not right now,' he said, and moved on.

All around him was disco. Surprisingly good disco. When you've lived through the twentieth century a few times over, you'll go to a lot of parties. Most of them a bit rubbish, really. When you come down to it, it's all a mixture of sex, chemicals, fancy hair, loud music, dry ice and, in the 1970s, roller skates.

For a large chunk of the twentieth century, Jack hadn't been drinking, and he'd never got the hang of roller skates. But he still fancied he knew how to twist up a rug, and this seemed pretty, well… A few parties stood out. He'd gone to the Cavern Club in Liverpool in the early 1960s to hear The Beatles' first-ever concert. Not so much cos he liked the music, but just in case He turned up. He never could resist a spot of showy nostalgia. Actually, He hadn't, but Jack had still had a surprisingly good time with a party of student nurses in Biba skirts.

Then there was that lost weekend in the Weimar Republic in the 1930s. Berlin loved to party, and those Germans – they really loved a man in uniform. He'd been supposed to be investigating rumours of trafficking in Alien Artefacts by some leading National Socialists, but had got distracted by… well, everything really. About the only thing he remembered was the look when he'd handed in his expenses claim.

Oh, and that party in an enormous warehouse in Docklands, way before it got redeveloped. Back then it was just an enormous shed of noise, with people draped across the stairs. The host lived in a greenhouse in the middle of the second floor and made weird films. The warehouse was breathtakingly cold and filthy, but everyone looked amazing. The music was bizarre, and every single mattress was crowded with beautiful people. Oh, and there had been cheese-on-sticks and fireworks along the Thames.

And then there was this. Someone had repainted the entire club a burning white, the walls glowing with the heat from the lights. The floor itself blazed with light, the entire club both full of shadows and yet having no shadow. The bar was a long plate of shining glass, with mirrors behind it, floating somehow above the dance floor. Tables of polished steel leaned against mirrored columns of solid light. Everything was bright and burned and the noise flowed up and around. Even the dry ice appeared to be glitter, floating around everyone like dusk in summer.

Jack made his way to the bar, and enjoyed the spectacle. Everyone was young, they were thin, they were pretty and happy. No one seemed drunk, just blissful. And nearly everyone was dancing.

He saw Brendan over in the DJ booth. He was standing there, just wearing a pair of combats and some headphones. His blond hair was flowing effortlessly free. He waved towards Jack, and Jack walked over.

'It's been a while!' Brendan said, his normal voice somehow

making itself heard over the crowd.

'There's been no need,' replied Jack.

'Forgive the appearance. I'm just dressed down tonight. You know how it is. Fancied a spot of DJ-ing. After all, everyone loves a DJ.' He winked. 'Let's go upstairs and get a drink with Jon.' He reached out of the booth and tapped a student wearing speedos and a snake tattoo. The boy turned and looked at Brendan and smiled. Brendan leaned down and stroked his arm. The boy stepped forward and they kissed in the booth. Brendan leaned away. 'What's your name?'

'Eric.'

'Good boy, Eric. You get to DJ. You'll do brilliantly.' Brendan kissed him again and walked away.

Jack shook his head. 'You two are worse than me.'

Brendan shrugged. 'You don't know the half of it.' He strode off.

Behind him, Jack's smile died.

Upstairs had never been much of a bar. Just kind of an overfill that occasionally did for functions or strip shows and Karaoke. But now it was all wood panelling and leather chairs and underfloor lighting.

As Jack walked in, Jon was walking over from the bar with three drinks. He smiled, happy to see the Captain.

'Do you like what we've done?' he asked.

Jack nodded. People sat on the couches, chatting and smiling. The bar appeared to sell vodka and toast. Somewhere, three bottle-blond kids from Swansea were poking uncertainly at some dim-sum.

Jack sat down at a little table. He could still hear the amazing noise from the club below. But also…

Over the PA, the barman announced, 'And next on Karaoke is Barry from Barry. And he'll be doing the Queen of the Night's song from *Die Zauberflöte*.'

Brendan giggled. 'Such a lovely boy. Great voice, but he'll never make that high G.'

As the Mozart thundered around them Jack blinked. Brendan laughed. 'Oh, the Opera Karaoke? All Jon's idea.'

'Well, life's not all party favours and Kylie,' said Jon. 'And it's a touch of class. It's not show tunes.'

'I've never been a fan of musical theatre,' said Jack.

Over on the Karaoke screen, the ball hopped its way across the words:

'Der Holle Rache kocht in meinem Herzen; *Hell's vengeance seethes in my heart;*

Tod und Verzweiflung flammet unm ich her! *The flames of death and despair engulf me…*'

Jack tried not to marvel as people put down their drinks and toast and started to join in in a boozy, heartening way.

Jon smiled. 'I know it's a bit campy, but we're very old gods. Anything goes. Well, apart from Harrison Birtwhistle. Would you begrudge us this?'

'Don't hurry him.' Brendan grinned. 'There's always a but with Jack. Hold that thought.'

'What?' asked Jon.

Brendan pointed. A kid wearing normal clothes and too much wet-look hair gel had wandered in. 'Underneath those baggy clothes and that home dye job, he's gorgeous. You can tell it's his first time out. In two minutes' time he's going to be smoking a granny fag outside and wishing he fitted in.'

Jon patted his partner on the arm. 'Go get him, tiger.'

Brendan gave a mock sigh of exhaustion. 'No rest for the wicked, you know how it is.' He winked, grabbed his drink and his cigarettes and, steering the kid by the shoulder, swept him outside.

Jon turned back to Jack. 'See? Another soul rescued. People

will see him with us. We're so beautiful, some of that rubs off on him. He'll make friends. He'll dress like them, someone will cut his hair. He'll sleep with a few of them, get his heart broken, get tougher, go down the gym, break a few hearts of his own… It's all good. Community service.'

Jack said nothing.

'Yeah. We've led by example. Oh, it's been a great few months.' Brendan laughed and ruffled Jack's hair. 'Seriously. We've made so many friends, we've improved the boys and the music. We've even raised house prices by a few per cent. Plus we've got laid loads. What's not to love?'

Jack sipped his drink, thoughtfully.

Jon shrugged. 'I know what you're going to say, but really, don't be a stranger. There's always a place in our hearts and our bed for you, Jack. You get me – I know what it's like. You're fighting Weevils, we're fighting off bears. But, look around you, sweetheart. Isn't this better than what there was? Look at how happy we've made everybody. Even the kids from Newport.'

Jack looked at him and smiled.

'Oh, I keep cutting you off, which is so annoying!' laughed Jon. 'What is the thing? Have you come for a bit of advice? Cos, if you don't mind me saying, the military retro thing has kind of gone. We need to get you in something tight and fitting. Some fabrics that'll breathe, if you know what I mean.'

Brendan came back to the table, smirking.

Jon glanced at him. 'You dirty slut,' he sighed.

Brendan puckered his mouth. 'Yeah, well, I made him happy – he'll have a great evening.'

Jon tutted. 'And you come back smelling of cheap fags. Can you not try out menthol?'

Brendan shuddered. 'It's like licking a minty road. No thanks. Now, Captain Jackoff – what can we do you with?' And he raised his eyebrows suggestively.

Jon shrugged. 'He's not said. Not really got a word in edgewise, have you? Silly me, I'm turning into such a gassy old Mary. It's the bloody Welsh. So gregarious. I swear they're rubbing off on me.'

He laughed in a nasal way, and Brendan growled at him.

'So, Jack, what have you come here to say? Are you going to congratulate us for everything we've done?'

Jack's smile faded. 'Nope. I'm here to take you in.'

'What?' Jon's cocktail paused mid-sip. Brendan reached nervously for his lighter.

'You heard. The show's over. You've broken our agreement. I was a fool to trust you. So now it ends.'

'Oh,' said Jon, a little sadly. 'You knew?'

'I'm only sorry it took me so long to notice!' exclaimed Jack, furiously angry. 'Why couldn't you have come to me earlier? We might have helped you. Instead people have died. And...' he looked truly regretful. 'I thought there were two people in Cardiff who really understood me, who I could trust... and now this. Sorry. Party's so over.'

Brendan let out a long-held breath. 'Fooo. OK. Wow. Bit sudden, but OK,' he said. 'We'll play by the rules, won't we, Jonno?'

'Yup,' said Jon, moving closer to Jack. 'Last dance, Captain?'

'Sure,' said Jack. 'Why not?'

And they led him to the dance floor. And a day passed.

THE PERFECTION DANCES IN MYSTERIOUS WAYS

'You were right,' whispered Jon in his ear. As they moved across the dance floor, people just stepped out of their way. 'You said Gods were just conmen with good technology.'

'And you were.'

Brendan pressed up against Jack's back, laughing. 'Oh we were good. So good. But the machine made us BETTER.'

'Oh,' sighed Jack. Partly cos he was understanding, partly because Brendan was gently kissing the back of his neck.

'We didn't need the machine, but we built it anyway. It made our life easier. Just as you don't need a dishwasher, but once you've got one…' explained Jon.

'Dishwashers? Jeez,' sighed Brendan in Jack's ear. 'Can you believe him?'

'What did your machine do?' asked Jack, trying to concentrate. The music, the lights – the feeling of the Perfection, wrapping themselves around him. The way they were all starting to move together, the way the music was getting louder, and yet further away, was somehow slowing down… were they even moving at all?

'It's a belief system. It made it easier for us to give our believers what they wanted. God created Man, and Man created God… you know…'

'You know,' repeated Brendan, mockingly in Jack's ear.

'It let us answer their prayers. It kept us perfect,' continued Jon. 'At the moment, for example, it lets me avoid wrinkles, and it keeps Brendan from losing his hair. Plus those love handles.'

'Shut up!' hissed Brendan.

'Oh, it's true. Ahhh, I love this bit!' Jon shouted as the music built up and hit them like a wave.

And, like a wave, suddenly everything for Jack was down, not up, then up, not down, then he gasped for breath. 'What's happening to me?' he asked. 'What's happening to me?' he shouted.

Was he alone on the dance floor? Could he even open his eyes? He shouted and shouted again and then—

'It's OK, sssh!' breathed Jon, kissing him. 'The music's just really good tonight. What is that kid DJ's name?'

'Eric,' replied Brendan.

'Oh, we're keeping him!' laughed Jon. 'Anyway, to business. Which is you, Captain.'

'So you had your machine,' said Jack. Was he slurring? Anyway. 'And you come to Cardiff and…'

'We just settled for a little bar, a nice flat, and for making everyone happy. That's all we did. Is that such a crime?' Brendan's voice took on a begging tone. And was he starting to glow slightly?

Jack blinked a bit, and tried to focus. Focus on making the—

'And then we lost it. It was stolen.'

'I know,' said Jack. God, he was sweating. 'They're right,' he thought. 'It's this coat. I'm wearing too many clothes. Giggle. Oh that's funny. Always wearing too many clothes.'

'Have you got it with you?' asked Brendan. 'No? OK. So we needed the device back. It was still being used, but at a long distance from us – the power it's been demanding has spiralled. We've done everything we could to feed it… but it's not been enough.'

'You should have asked me,' said Jack. 'We could have helped.'

'Maybe it's not too late,' said Jon.

'It is,' said Brendan. 'Gods have their pride.'

Jon leaned close.

'He's got really good arms,' thought Jack. 'He's so strong, and his hair's so good and I love the way his eyes are so blue and there's all that stubble and the troubled look in his face and the chest hair and cheekbones and—'

'Jack. Listen to me, Jack,' said Jon. 'We had to feed it. Using the old way.'

Brendan leaned in, his long blond hair sweeping back, his perfect teeth smiling in a feral way. His arms wrapped round Jack, so strong, almost crushing the life out of him.

'We've had to make sacrifices,' someone said.

And then it was white.

JACK IS IN FOR A TREAT WHEN HE CHECKS THE CCTV

Gwen awoke, chewing hair. She realised, gradually, that it wasn't hers, and woke with a guilty start.

She and Ianto were wrapped round each other on the Hub's battered sofa. Gwen remembered they'd worked through the night and then just sat down, just for a second, just to catch their breath. And… how late was it?

She jabbed Ianto in the ribs.

Ianto gave a sudden snore, and snapped awake. He gazed around, blearily. 'Gwen… what?' For an instant, his face was dishevelled, hair unkempt, clothes rumpled. Then he shook himself like a cat, and everything fell into place. Perfectly.

Gwen narrowed her eyes. 'Ianto! We've been asleep!'

Ianto stood up, and clumped unevenly towards his desk. 'I'm missing a shoe,' he muttered.

'Oh god, I'm so tired,' wailed Gwen. 'I haven't slept properly all week, and now this.'

Ianto checked the clock on his PC. 'We've been asleep for four hours. I just shut my eyes, just for a moment…' He smiled at Gwen, encouragingly. 'I'll make some coffee.'

Gwen stumbled over to her machine, and pulled up the latest reading of the energy cloud. It had increased, no, doubled, while they'd been asleep. She stared, aghast.

Ianto joined her, and they sat there for a few minutes, groggily, sipping their coffee and watching the world end.

'It's like a net,' sighed Ianto. 'Very tightly woven. Hovering just a few feet over Cardiff.'

Gwen nodded. 'And getting ready to drop.'

'Right,' said Ianto, firmly. 'We need to find Jack. And we need to get the device to him.'

'Right,' said Gwen. They sat there, watching the energy net weaving itself tighter and tighter.

'What's unique about Jack?' asked Ianto. 'We need something we can trace him by.'

'Oh, you can't track smugness,' said Gwen.

CAPTAIN JACK GOES TO THE WALL

Jack was pressed up against the wall, Brendan wrapped around him. He was wearing a drowsy, dreamy smile. 'What are we doing now, fellas?' he asked, his voice thick with sleep.

Jon moved across the room, and threw an arm around Jack's shoulder, drawing him close. 'Oh, it's all good, soldier.'

Jack blinked, slowly. 'Why… Why am I here?'

Brendan laughed, gently in his ear. 'You've forgotten! Oh, that's great.'

'We are very distracting,' said Jon.

'And haven't you done well?' said Brendan, admiringly.

'What?' murmured Jack. 'What have I done?'

'Provided us with a lot of much-needed power,' said Jon. 'You could call it a jump start.'

'Please don't,' sighed Brendan. He started to kiss Jack's neck. Jack laughed, slowly. 'Listen, babe, we've got to go for a few hours. And you're pretty much spent. So we're going to leave you here.'

'You'll like this bit,' said Jon. 'Spread out your hands.'

And Jack spread out his hands, feeling the two of them wrapped round him, and he smiled, happily. None of it felt real. He looked at the wall, all neat, white plaster, and then watched, dreamily, as it changed, spreading with a blood-red stain which moved around his figure. And then rippled. And the pounding, the pounding that had been in his head for so long he couldn't remember... oh, it got louder.

'It's the wall,' said Brendan, pressing in on him. 'Try and move your hands.'

Jack couldn't. He managed to lift his left hand, just slightly, but the wall shifted. He struggled, and the wall just wrapped itself further round his arm. He turned, almost alarmed, but still giggly. 'What is this?'

'It's the wall,' said Jon. 'We built a temple, after all.'

Brendan pulled close, kissing Jack and running a hand through his hair. 'We built it out of our believers.'

And then he broke away from Jack, laughing as they pushed him into the wall. As it wrapped round his head and his body, so warm and horrible and strange, he realised that something very bad had happened. And he tried to scream. But as he opened his mouth, the wall just poured in. All warm and pulsing and red.

IANTO KNOWS THE TRUE VALUE OF A NUGGET

Ianto stumbled through central Cardiff. The streets were eerily empty, bathed in the watered-down light of winter. Buses were still running, with exhausted drivers barely lifting their eyes from the road. Shops were open, but the music was muted. The streets were full of rubbish, coke cans and chip wrappers and bottles and even the odd person, slumped in a doorway.

'I'm so tired,' he thought. 'I'm so tired I could just sleep.'

He carried on walking, though. Down along St Mary Street, which was still crowded with clubbers, milling around in an exhausted, desultory way. He checked his watch, puzzled. It was either early or late. He couldn't work it out. It was almost like they'd left the clubs and not bothered to go home, just stayed on the street. Standing fairly still, staggering from side to side, a little. Almost like they were still dancing.

Every now and then a bottle would drop to the ground, and he'd hear it rolling a little.

He made his way through the crowd, finding the fish bar.

Bren caught his look, so old, so tired. 'Oh, we don't close while there's business, luv,' she said. 'Patrick's still out the back.' Her look wasn't approving. 'Don't distract him. He's got nuggets, hasn't he?'

'But he's OK?' asked Ianto.

Bren didn't even blink. 'Of course. Why shouldn't he be?'

Ianto swept through to the back of the shop, where Patrick stood, emptying an enormous sack of frozen chicken nuggets into a deep fat fryer. He turned and smiled at her.

'It's been a long night,' he said.

'A really long night,' Ianto agreed.

'And then you turn up,' Patrick sighed. 'Frankly, all I want is a nice bacon roll and a cup of tea and to go to bed.'

'Me too.'

'Really?' Patrick raised an eyebrow, amused. 'Beautiful women normally play harder to get.'

'Oh,' sighed Ianto. 'I didn't mean anything, really.'

'Of course you didn't,' Patrick smirked, and wiped his hands down on his apron. 'Anyway, guardian angel, I'm still alive. Which I guess means that we get to have that date.'

'Oh,' said Ianto. 'That's a good point.'

'So. When I finish work tomorrow?' he looked at Ianto, almost pleadingly.

'Of course,' said Ianto, a bit too quickly.

'Meaning?'

'Thank you for calling me beautiful,' Ianto said. His phone rang.

It was Gwen. She was excited.

'Right,' said Ianto. 'I'll be there in ten minutes, promise.'

He hung up and turned back to Patrick. 'Got to go. Sorry. You going to put your nuggets on, or what?'

ERIC DOESN'T FEEL LIKE DANCING, NO SIR, NO DANCING TODAY

The mewling woke him briefly

'Hey,' Jack said

'You're alive?' asked the mewling, amazed

'Always' he said, and he found that funny briefly

'Stop laughing! Stop! Please!' cried the mewling. 'You've been laughing for ten minutes. Please stop.'

OK, maybe he'd found it funny for a bit too long there

He wasn't really sure

But he was Captain Jack, he was a fun guy to be with

Fungi to be with. Was that ever funny? I guess it is now

Laugh again

He contemplated opening an eye, then decided it was too much like hard

Actually, really needed to pee

Should do something about that at some point soon

So, back to opening an eye

Coming back to life was always a struggle – maybe one day he just wouldn't be bothered and that would finally be it

Good thing/Bad thing?

Really need to pee, can't ignore it any more

The mewling started again

Eye open, finally, wince, that's really, really bright... Ride it out, Harkness, let's see where we

Oh

Not good

'Hey!' he said to the mewling. 'It's Eric isn't it?'

The DJ from the night before looked up (down?) at him. He was making an effort to stop crying, sniffing bravely like a child. 'Yeah.'

'Hi! Captain Jack Harkness!' Jack loved his back-up personality. Always there, glowing away faintly, lighting the way to the fire escape. 'I would shake you by the hand, but if I've still got one, I certainly can't move it.'

'Can you help us?'

'Again, I'd shrug if I could. I've got a good track record. How long have we been here?'

'Eight hours, I think. You've not moved for four.'

'Good watch, kid.'

'I've nothing else to do but count.'

'Hey, there's a copy of *Metro* in my coat pocket. I'd hand it over to you if I could move and if I had any clothes.'

'Thanks,' said Eric. 'I could leave you a message in the I Saw You column. "I saw you embedded in a wall, Tuesday. You looked back. Drink?"'

Jack laughed.

Eric looked at him sharply. Jack stopped laughing.

'How long was I laughing this time?'

'Eighty-seven seconds.'

'Close to mania. Curious.'

'And irritating.'

'Says crying man.'

'Hey, I'm in a lot of pain.'

'I can see that.'

'Can you? It's just that I can't move.'

'I can see that.'

'I can't feel my legs.'

'That's cos you've not got any.'

Pause. That was tactless.

More mewling. Some screaming.

'I mean, not that I can see. Stop crying. It's the wall – they're embedded in the wall behind you. Who knows. Probably all there. All fine. Looks worse than it is – seems to be concrete, but it's alive and breathing and… smells quite meaty. God knows, I mean, I'm sure it's all fine. I'm probably in a worse state.'

Now Eric laughed. 'Can't you see?'

'Not really, no. Can't move my neck.'

'Captain Jack Harkness, you're just a head. Well, a bit of torso.'

Back-up personality. Say something.

'Breasts? I never was much of a breast man, but if it's all I've got left… Even a nipple?'

Sudden thought. Is the need to pee real or illusory? Perhaps I should just let it go and see what happens. But then, what if the resulting sensation is both imaginary and gross?

I am in a wall.

GWEN WELCOMES CAREFUL DRIVERS

Gwen was starting to freeze. The rain was soaking through her coat, her trousers were sopping wet, and her hair was plastered to her head. 'What kept you?' she barked at Ianto as the SUV drove up. 'You said you'd be ten minutes.'

Ianto apologised hastily, but also shot her a look as she climbed in. 'Careful with that car seat, please, Gwen. I've just had the upholstery steam-cleaned.'

'Fine, Ianto, thank you, Ianto, I shall try and drip elsewhere. Where the bloody hell were you?'

Ianto looked slightly sheepish as he drove the SUV up from the Bay into town. 'Well, when you called, I suddenly realised it might be a long night, and I didn't want that on an empty stomach, what with my blood sugar being all over the place these days, so I zapped a Lean Cuisine and counted my points while I waited. Honestly, I got here as quickly as I could. Oh, plus I had to find the keys to the SUV.'

Gwen sat there quietly. In less than a week, not only had Ianto become a woman, but he'd become the kind of woman Gwen always dreaded being behind at a cashpoint.

'You count your points? Don't tell me you're doing Weight Watchers?' Gwen was slightly aghast. Ianto's figure was perfect. Unquestionably so.

They pulled up at the lights, and Ianto turned to Gwen, smiling gently. 'Not religiously, no, but it's a good idea to eat sensibly, Gwen. I mean, I know you're married and it's easy to get...'

The smallest pause.

'... comfortable. But if it turns out I'm stuck in this body, I've got to look my best. I'm a single woman, remember.'

Gwen blinked. She could have sworn the car smelt of chips.

Meanwhile, Ianto checked his hair in the rear-view mirror and completely missed the lights changing until the bus behind them sounded its horn.

Ianto then stalled the SUV, swore mildly, and roared off in the wrong gear. 'Honestly! The clutch keeps getting away from me. These shoes are bloody murder to drive in,' he cursed. 'I just can't get shoes right. Either that or someone keeps moving the seat. Now, are you sure this device will work?'

Gwen pulled it from her coat pocket. It was sleek, blue and bleepy. 'Tosh designed it for hunting Weevils, based on the scents they emit during the mating cycle. According to her notes, she had a few false starts with tom cats, but it's now pretty good at hunting them down when they're randy.'

'Aw, Tosh had the sweetest hobbies.' Ianto smiled fondly. 'Did it make sense of the stuff I gave you?'

Gwen checked the readings. 'Pretty much. You were right – Jack's fifty-first-century pheromone pattern is fairly distinctive. It's just not very strong. Even around the Hub. So our best hope of finding him is to stick this out the window and drive round Cardiff city centre very slowly.'

Ianto fumbled a crunching gear change and brought them to a juddering halt.

'Shouldn't be too much of a problem,' Gwen muttered, winding down the window.

CARDIFF IS A ONE-WAY CITY

Town was even worse than earlier. Someone was slumped across every bench, or, in some cases, just stretched out across the pavement. Exhausted pensioners sat slumbering at bus stops. Rain beat down mercilessly on cars, buildings and people. Traffic crawled sluggishly, causing Gwen to scream with frustration.

'It's this new one-way system,' she howled.

'Or the end of the world,' said Ianto.

'Whatever.' Angrily, she shook the tracking device which refused even to bleep.

The lights changed and the SUV slid glacially forward in the traffic.

'Look at the sky, Gwen,' said Ianto, sadly.

Gwen looked, and didn't like it. Cardiff had its fair share of menacing clouds, but these were biblical in their darkness. Pushing down on the buildings, boiling angrily away, pouring rain down on the city.

'That doesn't look good,' Gwen sighed.

The car crawled along a few hundred metres, and suddenly the tracking device screamed like a toddler.

'Bloody hell!' Gwen yelped, waving it around. She frantically adjusted the settings and the screaming subsided. 'It's over there,' she pointed. 'Jack's over there.'

Ianto took the tracker and stared at the screen. 'What can have produced that many pheromones? That's off the scale, even by Jack's standards.'

'I know,' said Gwen, grimly. 'We've got to get to him.'

'Charles Street,' said Ianto. 'It'll be a few minutes before we can get back round the one-way system.'

'Sod that,' snapped Gwen. 'Just park on the pavement.'

BOUNCER BEN IS WONDERING WHY HIS NOSE GOT BROKEN

It had been a long night. Actually, it seemed to have gone on for… well, Ben wasn't quite sure, but he was quite snug, really. Even in the pouring rain, he was wrapped up warm, and the heat fairly blasted out of the club's doors along with the music, which, although it wasn't normally his kind of thing, he had to admit, was pretty spectacular. He'd work at the Temple for free, if it meant listening to the music. Of course, he was too wise to say that kind of thing. Professional pride. But he liked to think they knew.

And since he'd turned his phone off, his wife had stopped ringing him to demand he come home.

Something was wrong with that sentence. Hmm.

He snapped awake as he heard steps on the metal stairs above him. He watched as two women walked down them. One was startlingly beautiful and having trouble with her shoes. The other was holding out a small blue phone thing. He decided it was best to look business.

The beautiful one stepped up. 'Hello, mate,' she said, surprisingly. 'Two, please. We'd like to disco very much.'

Her companion glanced at her in something like shock and then turned to Ben. 'How much, please?'

Ben looked at them both. 'I'm sorry. It's a private party.'

The stunning one leaned closer and smiled. Ben noticed her friend was rolling her eyes. 'Oh come on now, surely you can make an exception for us? We're always where the party's at.'

The other one stepped forward. 'Thing is, see, we've got a friend in there, we said we'd join him and…' She made to step through, but Ben moved easily out to block her.

He looked at them both, patiently. Lasses like this, it was worth telling it to them frankly. He put on his firmest voice. He knew what it was like – a night out on the lash, few too many bottles of blue alco-piddle, kebab, loud vows to party on past dawn. He'd had nearly eight years of it, and was an expert in turning people gently but firmly away.

'Now listen, ladies, why don't you go home and have a cup of tea?' he began, talking first to the tall, stunning one. 'Now, you – pretty girl like you, this isn't really your place to find a fella. Waste of effort, if you know what I mean. And you,' he said, turning to the second woman, not unkindly. 'Well, I'm afraid we've got our quota of fag hags.'

Gwen broke his nose.

IANTO IS JUST MURDER ON THE DANCE FLOOR

They stood on the threshold of the club for a few moments, unable to believe what they were seeing.

Torchwood had shown Gwen a lot of things. She'd seen a fair bit of carnage inside, outside and underneath nightclubs. This was unlike anything she'd ever seen. Even when she was young and going to festivals in Fungus's camper van. This was…

She remembered being a bit stoned and leaving the folk tent, getting a falafel and then accidentally wandering into the techno tent. This was the nearest thing – suddenly plunged into a dark place filled with endless noise and bodies and lights and screaming and a vague feeling of panic and revulsion mixed with a wonder about how she could ever fit in and be cool here.

The club, with its blood-red walls and mirrors and lights seemed to stretch into infinity. The dance floor was packed, packed with topless men all dancing, dancing the same little dance moves, all at the same time, all of them staring ahead, their muscles twitching, their eyes white, looking like racks and racks of meat in a disco abattoir. Just moving to the beat, swinging like they were on rows of meat hooks. Just empty meat dancing and dancing and dancing.

Sweat dribbled down the mirrors and columns and pooled on the ceiling and the floor. She could see the odd figure, passed out but propped up by those dancing around it. Slack jaw staring at the ceiling, collecting drops of sweat.

She thought briefly of that YouTube clip of hundreds of prisoners all doing synchronised dancing to Michael Jackson. It was kind of like that. Only crammed in all together, and the guys were semi-naked and really, really hot.

The smell was incredible. It was an actual proper stench – of hundreds of different types of sweat, of stale dry ice, of spilt beer, of decay and death and blood.

And then she noticed the pulsing music, the way the walls, the lights, the twitching bodies were all pulsing like a heartbeat. Regular, somehow sickening.

Ianto turned to her. 'This could be heaven, this could be hell,' he breathed. All he could see was row after row of beautiful people, somewhere near a state of rapture. And the music and the music and the beat and the lights and the music and—

Gwen slapped him. Pretty hard, he thought.

'Sorry,' said Gwen flatly.

'Thank you,' he replied rather crisply. 'It's strangely… compelling.'

Gwen shrugged. 'Oh, I dunno. Dancing, I can take it or leave it, me. But look at all this. What the hell do we do?'

Ianto paused. 'They're behaving like a mass. They're just standing there – not even lifting a foot off the floor. We should find what's causing that. Perhaps we could stop that.'

'Yep,' agreed Gwen.

'We could find Jack. See if he can help.'

'Also good,' said Gwen.

'We could also find out why the walls are breathing.'

'Um. Yeah.'

Actually, they made their way awkwardly to the bar. No one seemed to notice them. Everyone was dancing, dancing, dancing, their eyes rolled up, enraptured.

Gwen giggled. 'It's like the nineties, but no one's tried to hug me or backwashed in my water bottle.'

Ianto nodded. 'I've been to parties like this too. But normally in abandoned warehouses. Not, you know, on Charles Street.'

The pounding was starting to really beat down on Gwen. She looked at the DJ, who was mixing away at his desk, but without even looking at it. It was really, really creepy. As she leaned on the bar she sensed the beat travelling through her. She tried to move and found it harder than she thought, as though the surface of the bar was really, really sticky. She finally got the attention of a barman, who beamed at her glassily. 'What'll it be?' he asked.

'Are you the manager?' she asked.

He shook his head. 'He's on holiday, really. Upstairs.'

'Who's in charge?'

He shook his head again. 'The music's in charge.'

Gwen rolled her eyes. She could see Ianto leaning forward, trying to flirt with the other barman who, frankly, had too many muscles and too small a T-shirt to be really interested. Bless, she thought. She turned back to the barman. 'Look – who is in charge? Who pays you?'

The man looked puzzled. 'We haven't been paid. We're here for the love. The power.' He grinned suddenly, raffishly, and then started to bang his head to the music, drifting gently away.

Ianto joined her. 'Nothing. It's like I'm invisible.'

Finally!

Gwen nudged towards the fire escape. 'Let's go out to the smoking garden,' she said, and strode off, edging around the side of the club, past untouched drinks and a group of men who were leaning back against the wall, dancing as though stuck to it. All of them wore the same lopsided grin.

The smoking garden was creepy. It was packed, but no one was smoking.

At each table in the freezing night sat boys in T-shirts, their hands clasped around long-dead cigarettes. All of them were just staring ahead, nodding in time to the beat.

'Seriously, seriously wrong,' said Gwen, watching as the rain plopped into unguarded drinks.

'Wrong and creepy,' agreed Ianto. He reached into his enormous handbag and pulled out a tiny pop-up Snoopy umbrella. They huddled under it and watched the sodden crowd.

Gwen peeped out from under the umbrella. A fire escape led up to a second floor. She pointed it out. 'I was told the manager had gone on holiday upstairs,' she said.

'Yeah,' agreed Ianto. 'They said something about a Brendan and a flat.' He checked his PDA. 'There's nothing about a Brendan here on the records. We should be looking for a manager called Rudyard.'

'Rudyard?' laughed Gwen. 'No one is called Rudyard.'

Ianto held up the PDA. 'Here he is. He's got a beard and everything.'

'Right,' admitted Gwen. 'Well done, Miss Jones. Ten Points to Hufflepuff. Now come on – let's climb up the fire escape. If Jack's here, I bet that's where he'll be.'

Ianto pointed in alarm at his shoes and Gwen smiled. 'Honestly, Ianto, nearly a week and you still haven't learned – it's practical pumps for missions.'

Ianto winced. 'I know, Gwen, but these look so good.'

Gwen patted him on the shoulder. 'It's a sacrifice worth making. I'll give you a bunk up.' And so, in the rain and the music, Gwen found herself hoisting Ianto's ankles onto a rusty ladder.

CAPTAIN JACK IS BARGAINING

'What is this?' Jack asked Brendan.

Brendan, pottering past with a piece of toast, paused and ruffled his hair. 'It's got many names. Call it our Belief System. It's a way of bonding all our true believers together, giving us the power we need to do all our good deeds.'

'It's obscene,' growled Jack.

Brendan offered him a bite of toast. Jack shook his head. 'You're only saying that cos you're on the inside looking out. I think it's all rather beautiful. It's kind of like the tar baby. And it's only a temporary solution until we can find that machine.'

'It's not working. Let me out of this – I can help you,' said Jack.

'Pleading?' Brendan squatted down, meeting Jack's eyes. 'It's rather beneath you, Captain.'

'Not if it saves lives,' said Jack.

Brendan rolled his eyes. 'You are so noble, I could eat you up. Sure you don't want some toast?'

'What would be the point?' sighed Jack. 'How long are you going to keep me here?'

Brendan shrugged. 'Dunno. In a few hours we might let you all out for a bit and play with you. Depends how up for it Jon is. Then we'll pop you all back in. Cos I've got yoga, and I can't leave you all alone with Jon. He might go mad.'

'You know that's not what I meant.'

'Truthfully, until we get the device back. The problem is, our need for power's growing at a rate… oh, I dunno. It's a bit worrying. Frankly, I think we'll be running out of boys soon. Which isn't a great state of affairs really, is it? We might have to reach out wider and wider. You know, Aberdare.'

'Can't you see how stupid this is?' gasped Jack.

'Totally,' admitted Brendan. 'But it's what we've got to do to stay alive, to carry on searching, to find that bloody thing. Trust me, Jack, I'm a god. It's what we've got to do to stay alive. When we get our power back, we'll make everything right again.'

Jon walked into the room, towelling himself after a shower. 'You all right babe?' he asked Brendan.

'Yeah,' said Brendan.

Jon flicked Jack playfully with the towel. 'Are you talking to the furniture again?'

'Stop this!' said Jack.

Jon arched an eyebrow. 'You don't look happy Jacky,' he said, squeezing Jack's cheek. Jack growled at him. Jon laughed and dropped the towel over Jack's head, leaving him fuming.

'Come on Bren, let's get some clothes on and go and see how things are downstairs.' They walked away, laughing, and all Jack could see was cotton.

RUDYARD IS SADLY ALL MOUTH

Gwen slid the window up, and the two of them slipped into a dark, quiet corridor.

'It's bloody great to be out of that rain,' shivered Ianto. 'I really miss jeans.'

'Well,' hissed Gwen, 'why don't you wear some?'

'Oh, it just hasn't felt right, really,' said Ianto. 'You know, I just don't think I've got the figure for them. I worry they'll make my bum look fat and squidgy.'

'Oh, bollocks,' hissed Gwen. 'You've got a lovely pair of child-bearing hips on you.'

'Have I?' Ianto looked genuinely pleased. 'Oh, that's nice.'

'Now, shut up, princess, and let's get on with it.'

The two of them started down the corridor, the flashlight gently glinting around them.

It all looked very dark, and the *thump-thump* of the club became overwhelming.

'Considering everything I've heard about gay grooming, it really reeks of BO in here,' said Ianto.

'Yeah,' agreed Gwen. 'Smells like a teenager's bedroom.'

Ianto pulled the pheromone sniffer out of his pocket and waved it around. 'Well, bloody hell,' he breathed. 'Jack's off the scale.'

Gwen cast her torch around the corridor. 'I'm not sure I like this,' she said.

They both heard the voice calling for help. It was a quiet voice, almost a whisper. Both jumped.

'Jeez!' wailed Gwen. 'I'm switching on the bloody light.' She fumbled her hand along the wall. 'Blimey, they've papered it with that velvet stuff they use at Indian restaurants,' she said, her hands brushing along the warm, slightly damp surface. 'It's like moss.' Her fingertips brushed up against what felt like a socket, and she reached out for the switch, but instead she felt something move and her hand went into the wall, into something warm and wet and—

it licked her.

She screamed and screamed and screamed, feeling it bite down.

Ianto ran up to her, his flashlight showing her hand embedded in a mouth in the wall.

Both shrieked.

'Do something!' wailed Gwen, helplessly.

'I don't want to touch it!' yelled Ianto.

'You're bloody squeamish when it suits you! It's biting me!' shouted Gwen.

'But it's a ... mouth... in a wall! It's wrong!'

'I don't care, it bloody hurts!' Gwen was starting to cry. Ianto tried pulling her by the arm, but Gwen just shrieked more. Ianto let go and stood back, hands on hips, trying to work out what to do, trying to block Gwen's shouts.

He noticed something – something oddly wrong. And then he saw the light switch, and flicked it.

Pause.

Gwen and Ianto were in a corridor of flesh – the walls were a kind of thick, coarse meat, breathing and rippling. Lumps and occasional limbs protruded at various points, fleshy trails hanging down from the ceiling, twitching slightly. Apart from the mouth that was eating Gwen's hand, there was the back of a head further down the corridor, and an ear.

'Can you switch the light back off?' hissed Gwen.

'No,' replied Ianto. 'This is just so horrible.'

'It's still eating my sodding hand!' wailed Gwen.

'Oh, sorry,' said Ianto. He grabbed a biro from his handbag and jabbed it into the mouth. 'Gag reflex,' he explained as Gwen pulled her hand out, gasping with the pain. 'I don't suppose you brought some Dettol?' she asked.

Ianto was just staring at the mouth, which was mouthing 'Help me' over and over again.

Gwen shook him. 'Come on.'

She dragged him down the corridor, both of them recoiling from the carpet, which appeared to be made up of matted human hair, streaking in colours and patterns and whorls and lumps through to a door.

The door, embedded as it was in meat, appeared to be a normal little Victorian-effect door, with a shiny gold handle. She pushed it open and, without thinking, flicked a switch on the right.

This room was worse. She stepped into it.

Ianto followed her, and breathed out raggedly. 'A Living Room. Oh my god.'

It had once been a quite nicely decorated, minimalist room – all white paint and polished floorboards. But it was now covered with lumpen flesh, twisting and veined across the walls, occasionally bursting out in cancerous bulges, or half-recognisable shapes. The whole room flowed across and hung away from a big bed, the covers turned down, the pillows scattered randomly about.

Tufts of hair poked up through gaps in the floorboards.

'I am going to be sick,' announced Gwen, starting to look round for somewhere to hurl.

'Gwen?'

She recognised Jack's voice and spun. She and Ianto ran towards a shape, roughly the size of a grand piano and covered with a dust sheet.

Ianto pulled away the sheet, and they both gasped.

'Ladies!' beamed Jack. He was, to their horror, entwined, impossibly entwined, in a heap of about sixteen naked men, enmeshed in the floorboards and protruding into the wall. When Hieronymus Bosch sat down to paint Hell, he'd left out the bit where they played Twister.

'Jack…!' began Ianto. He tasted vomit, swallowed, and went silent.

Gwen's reaction was different.

'Captain Jack Harkness!' she barked. 'When will you learn that you can't solve a problem by shagging it?'

'Hey!' said Jack, managing a shrug. 'It's a one-size-fits-all solution.' His expression shifted under Ianto's basilisk glare. 'Ianto! This isn't what it looks like. Have you met my friends Eric, Adam and Tristan, wasn't it?'

'Hi,' said some voices.

'Nice to meet you, I'm sure,' said Ianto crisply. 'Do I actually ask for an explanation or just take pictures for the album?'

Jack clucked, disapprovingly. 'This genuinely isn't an orgy. We're simply fuelling a vastly complicated energy exchange through the violent excitation of our biomass.'

'Uh-huh,' said Gwen. 'That would be the obvious explanation.'

'Seriously,' said Jack. 'It's an attempt to power that alien device. But it's not working well.'

'Evidently,' Ianto looked like he was chewing bees.

Jack sighed. 'This is serious. You need to do something. We're approaching critical mass.'

'Riiiight.' Gwen giggled. 'Oh, Jack, what a mess.'

'I tried to stop it. I failed,' Jack told them. 'It's got out of hand. I don't think they know what to do. Have you got—' And then: 'They're coming!'

The room's fleshy walls bulged, parted and extruded, swelling and tearing as the Perfection strode through.

They were both looking their best, gloriously naked. The entire meat of the room just shuddered.

Brendan nodded at them, crossed to the kitchenette and lit a cigarette from a packet on the table.

Jon walked over to Gwen and Ianto. 'How did you get in?' he demanded.

'Fire escape,' said Gwen.

'Ah,' said Jon. 'It's just that we've got psychic shielding up.'

'Is that so?' said Gwen. 'Only we're Torchwood.'

'Jack's friends.' Jon smiled at Jack. 'Well, it's sweet that you tried a rescue, but it's not going too well. And I don't believe that you got through our shields without help.' He turned to look at Ianto. 'And you – you've been touched by the machine. You're wearing Christine.' He ran a finger across Ianto's hair, and Ianto tried not to flinch. 'She suits you. Lovely work. It's not lost its touch. Where is it?'

Ianto had recognised their voices. These were the balls of fire. Those cruel, sing-song voices. They'd torn apart that boat in their fury, they'd wrecked lives looking for that machine, and they'd thrown up this unholy horror around them, all to show off their dreadful power. And now one of them was staring him in the eye and smiling slowly.

Bren looked up, tapping ash out. 'Have you brought us back the machine?'

'Would it actually help?' asked Ianto.

'It'd stop all this,' Brendan waved his cigarette around the room.

'Really? Could it make all these people better?'

'Oh probably. It can do all that, and make us gods again, and give you back Captain Jack. Lovely.' Brendan considered.

'And maybe that's the right thing. Or maybe this is our wake-up call.'

'What do you mean?' asked Jon.

'Why should the party stop? With the machine, we could expand again.' Brendan had stood up, spreading out his hands. 'Gods need room to breathe.' He started to glow.

'I think you should stop,' said Ianto, very quietly.

'What?'

'Just once, wouldn't it be nice to just go back to how things were? Everything's changed. But what about a bit more of the same?'

'I agree with the skirt,' shouted out Jack. 'I think you're both in danger of doing something very, very stupid.'

Jon shot him a glance. 'Looking like that, you manage that sentence?'

'I am not without a sense of irony,' muttered Jack.

Brendan advanced towards Ianto. 'Give us back the machine.'

'No,' said Ianto. 'I don't think it's safe in your hands any more.'

'Really?'

'No.'

Jon reached out a hand and, barely moving, he gently picked up Gwen and threw her screaming into the wall. She stuck fast, half in, half out, her hair sucked and pulled back. She screamed and struggled and only succeeded in vanishing further in.

Jack screamed back at Gwen. Ianto ran from the room.

Behind him he could hear the Perfection laughing.

IANTO JONES COULD TEACH YOU, BUT HE'D HAVE TO CHARGE

Ianto sat on the fire escape, sobbing to get his breath back. He opened up his handbag, and took out the bag with the alien device inside.

'Oh, you,' he thought. 'You've caused so much trouble. What the hell do I do now?'

He opened the bag, and tipped the device into his hand.

Captain Jack Harkness, at your service! Boomed a very familiar voice in his head.

'Why are you doing that?'

I'm the voice of who you most admire, Ianto Jones. Great shoes, by the way.

'Thanks. But I wish you wouldn't do him.'

Oh, come on, Ianto. It's just a bit of fun. Puts you at ease, doesn't it? Admit it. Just a little?

'It's comforting, yes. But it's not right. You shouldn't sound like him. Not when I'm trying to work out what to... do...'

It's really easy.

'Is it? Can you make everything right? Can you? Jack and that room and me?'

Yes. Trust me, Ianto.

'I'm not sure I can. I've seen what those creatures did looking for you.'

But Ianto – all the people I've helped. I helped so many on that boat.

'But so many people died. And look at me.'

I can fix you. And Jack. I can fix him too.

'NO!'

You love him. He doesn't love you. You saw him in there. But I can change all that, Ianto Jones.

'How can I trust you? Those creatures in there. They relied on you, and you—'

That's different. They were boring.

'What?'

I got bored. I always did. A few thousand years of perfection, and I'd make them move on. You know how it is. You cure war, famine, plague and pestilence and then… you know… it's the small stuff. I'm better off moving on. Like that Littlest Hobo doggy. Who doesn't love a dog?

'Again, what?'

I got bored. I made them come here. I thought it'd be a change. And I just wanted to move among you. When Ross and Christine stole me, I went willingly. And the Rift's made me so powerful. It's been brilliant. Mending lives – you people are so broken. I've lived on worlds where people had far less, led simpler lives and were so much happier. But look at you – you've got warm, dry homes, food, shops with Lego. And you're all miserable. I don't want to go back.

'I'm not sure you've got a choice,' said Ianto.

The machine sighed.

'Can you do what I want you to?'

Yes. There was a petulant note.

'It's asking a lot.'

Trust me, it'll be pretty spectacular. It'll be like the Bonfire Night and New Year's Eve all rolled into one.

'I love a show, me.'

Ianto climbed back inside, and strode down that horrifying corridor to the door. He could sense the entire house breathing around him.

It's not too late, you know. Would Jack do this? Ask yourself that.

'I don't care about that.' He shook his head. 'I am Ianto Jones and this is how I roll.'

He straightened his skirt, reached for his gun and kicked open the door.

IANTO IS CIVILISATION. END OF.

'Oh come off it,' snapped Brendan, clearly unimpressed by the gun. 'You barge back in here in your little black dress and expect us to be amazed.'

'Yes,' said Ianto.

'Do you know what we can do?' sneered Jon, stretching out an arm.

Ianto suddenly smelt burning hair and shuddered.

'Yes,' he said. 'And I don't care. I would like you to stop all this. And I would like Jack back.'

An outraged shriek.

'Oh, and Gwen too, please.'

Brendan laughed. 'We're too late for this. Jon, honey, we're getting old when we're being menaced by a little girl with a gun. Just give us the machine, dear.'

'We can do this the easy way, or the hard way,' said Ianto, quietly.

'Given the look of you, easy.'

'Seriously. Last chance. Dismantle this room.'

Jon shook his head, almost sadly. 'We can't. It's the machine – it's taking so much power. We have to feed it.'

'And that's always been the problem, hasn't it?' said Ianto. 'All those years, all those believers – it's all just fuel for that machine.

You've become enslaved by it.'

'Yes,' said Brendan quietly. 'I suppose we have.'

Jack started to laugh. 'You told me you were gods. Well, now we know what gods worship.'

'Yes,' snapped Jon. 'Perfection. And we had it when we had the device. Now look at it – we simply did this to try and make everything right. We were acting in the best interests.'

'Even gods lie to themselves,' said Jack sourly.

Ianto spoke quietly. 'I've talked to the machine.'

Brendan marched towards him.

'You've got it? You've got it on you? You silly bitch. You're not leaving the room with it.' He raised a glowing hand to strike Ianto.

Ianto fired and Brendan fell back, whimpering.

Ianto turned to Jon. 'I'm sorry. Would you also like to come and have a go? Are you feeling lucky? I am. I have your god on my side.'

He held up the device in its shiny plastic bag.

'Don't!' shouted out both Jack and Brendan.

'Ianto!' continued Jack. 'Don't touch it – it knows you're shutting down its power source. It will do anything it can to make you obey it. I don't care what it's offered you – it's lying, trying to get its way.'

'He's right!' barked Jon. 'It's the Lord of Lies. Why didn't we see it?'

'Because you were too busy looking in the mirror,' snapped Jack.

'Please,' said Brendan. 'Give us back the machine. Let us reset it. We can put everything right.'

Ianto shook his head. 'Nope, sorry. Made a deal. It told me how much power it needed. And that it had to come from somewhere. And I'm looking at you.'

Brendan went to stand by Jon's side. 'You are kidding me.'

'It giveth, and now, it tells me, it's ready to taketh away.'

'Wait!' snapped Brendan.

'Sorry,' said Ianto, and pushed the button.

And the world went white and changed a little.

EMMA WEBSTER IS STARTING AFRESH

'Would you like something to drink?'

Emma snapped to and flashed the waiter an apologetic look. She'd been daydreaming again, or something. The last few days were a bit of a blur. Like she'd just been asleep or taken something. Or something. She couldn't quite…

'Sparkling water, please.'

There. The waiter was gone. She had a couple more minutes to… it was like a memory that itched and itched and itched, but she just couldn't find it to scratch it. Wonder what it is. Wonder. She traced her hands over the tablecloth, watching the pattern.

Oddly, she couldn't even remember how she'd got to the restaurant, or why she was here. Maybe she'd just been born, just now, right here, and this was it. The first day of the rest of her life.

Only, she could clearly remember something really funny happening at work. She could remember Kate coming in, looking all fat, with her breast implants leaking during the management meeting. She'd cried and Emma had handed her a tissue. That had been funny. But she couldn't remember anything else about work. Perhaps she should get a different job. Yeah. Something fun.

Talking of fun, she was in a restaurant, she must be hungry.

Mind you, better watch the figure. Only, actually, looking pretty damn good, Miss Webster. I think starter and a pudding. She looked at the menu. Good, she appeared to be in a fish restaurant. She ran her fingers down the starters and lingered over the squid. Something tickled her leg. She looked down, and there was a cat, making its slow way round the tables, greeting the diners. She stroked it, and it nuzzled her back, giving her a look. She laughed and, as she laughed, she caught sight of the man standing by her table. Woah. Epic boy totty.

'Hi, is it Emma?' he said.

She stood up without falling over and said, 'Yes'.

But she wasn't quite sure in what order. Hum. He had a really great face. You know, the kind of face that, if it didn't belong to someone actually famous in *Heat*, definitely belonged to their boyfriend. It was a face that said confident, fun, shopping in New York, snowboarding and beach huts. He also looked pretty good in a suit. Really, just standing there staring now. Say something.

'And you are?' That was lame.

He gave her a bit of an embarrassed grin. 'I'm Patrick. Patrick Matthews.' Suddenly he scratched the back of his head and frowned. 'Sorry, like you care, too much detail. Just Patrick.' He deepened the frown. 'Never Pat.'

'Never,' she vowed. 'And?'

He looked a bit blank. 'I'm, uh, well… My friend Ianto, she set this up. I'm your blind date.'

'You are?' What? 'I mean, you are?'

He looked around, sheepish and slightly angry. 'Er, yeah. Complex story. Why, is something wrong?'

Emma giggled and suddenly felt really, really good. 'No, absolutely nothing. Sit down, and let's order a bottle of wine.'

He relaxed and suddenly looked even prettier. 'This is nice. Really nice.'

'Yes, yes it is.' Emma got distracted by the menu again. And a sudden thought. Who the hell is Ianto? And since when was that a girl's name?

He peeped over her menu, grinning at her. 'Red or white? Or shall we just get a bottle of pink fizz?'

'Oh,' she said, truly happy. 'That'll be perfect.'

At a table in the corner, Gwen relaxed and turned to Rhys. 'I think they'll be fine,' she said. 'You remember the drill?'

Rhys nodded solemnly. 'At the first sign of him turning into a skeleton, I'm to let you know.'

Gwen smiled approvingly. 'Good boy. Now what happened to my bread roll?'

Rhys brushed some crumbs off his jacket and shrugged. 'I thought you were leaving it. Sorry.'

Gwen decided she didn't actually care. It was a nice, warm night, and it looked like she was going to get through an entire meal out with Rhys without explosions, deaths or Weevils. She even risked slipping off her heels and letting her feet breathe. 'You know what?' she said. 'This place isn't actually that bad.'

'No,' agreed Rhys, polishing off the last of her roll.

And across town, Tombola's was as empty as usual. Until, suddenly, twelve customers materialised out of thin air. And they were all as mad as hell.

MADONNA IS A GAY ICON FOR BEGINNERS

Jack looked round the nightclub, a little sadly.

For a Saturday night, it was early, but still rather quiet. The bar staff sulked in a corner, polishing some glasses, texting, and generally ignoring him.

He turned to Ianto. 'It's a bit sad, in a way, you know.'

Ianto nodded gently. He had been working through a clipboard, ticking things off happily. He was now watching a Welsh digital channel on the flat-screen. 'It's true what they say, you know. You can never have enough about hill farming.'

Jack finally got served, and he carried their drinks over to a table that was sticky with spilt pints.

Ianto sipped his wine and grimaced. 'This is vile.' He ticked a box on the clipboard.

'I did warn you to stick to spirits,' said Jack. 'The worst they can do is water them down.' He sighed again, looking round the room. 'Could you not have left it a little fabulous?'

Ianto shook his head. 'Sorry. No. Look, it was a fairly major operation getting the machine to untangle all those body parts and make everyone normal. Even so, there's some poor kid in Barry who's missing a finger.'

Jack shrugged. 'Not our worst day. Memories?'

Ianto nodded happily. 'Completely wiped. Never had less

trouble getting people to take Retcon. I just told them all it was E.'

'You are going to hell, Ianto Jones.'

'Yes, Jack. But I'll still make a very pretty corpse.'

'That you will. Although there's some stubble showing.'

Ianto nodded, beaming. 'Oh yes. Last night as a woman according to the machine. Yay.'

They clinked their glasses.

'Gwen's already arranged to pop round tomorrow and steal all my clothes.'

'Good old Gwen.'

'So what about them?' Ianto gestured to a couple sitting quietly in a corner.

They were old, almost impossibly so, shrivelled in their clothes, which hung raggedly off them, far too young and fashionable for them. Each was clutching a glass of water and looking at nothing in particular. One had the wispy remains of fine blond hair. The other sported a random thatch of dark hair. You could somehow tell they'd once been devastatingly attractive.

Jack raised his glass to them, and they looked away.

'Sad,' he sighed. 'Not everyone gets a happy ending.'

'So is that it for the Perfection?'

'Pretty much. Completely disconnected from whatever powers they had, pumped full of Retcon. Seemed the kindest thing, really. I mean, would you want to remember? So they're now just mutton dressed as chicken.'

Ianto sighed quietly. 'They were gods once. They shaped worlds, ruled empires... and now they're just growing old, trapped in Cardiff.'

'As I said,' said Jack, sipping his drink, 'not everyone gets a happy ending.'

They left the club when the Karaoke started. As they headed for the door, a drag queen tottered onto the stage and began a Cher medley. A lesbian couple joined in, brokenly. And a strange little man in a cap shuffled onto the dance floor and, entirely for his own happiness, began to do the Running Man dance.

'All's right with the world,' sighed Jack as he sailed through the door.

Jack and Ianto stood on Charles Street, watching the evening go by.

A hen party staggered past, their progress impeded by the number of limbs that were in plaster. A voice screamed, 'Come on, Kerry, you dozy tart. Zambuca's not going to be 2 for 1 forever you know…'

Ianto watched them go, smiling broadly. 'Come on,' he said. 'Let's go down the Bay. I've got a promise to keep.'

And so they walked, in silence, until they came to a bridge overlooking a large amount of sea.

Ianto handed a small, glowing bag to Jack. 'Can you do this?' he asked. 'I'm not sure I trust myself. If I touch it again, I might ask it to do something.'

'And you're sure this is what it wants?' asked Jack.

'Yes. Just some peace. It's bored too, I think.'

'OK then,' said Jack. And he reached into the bag and pulled out the machine, which glowed happily in his hand. For an instant, it seemed like Jack was listening to a voice.

'Is it offering you anything?' asked Ianto, anxiously.

'Nope,' said Jack. 'Already perfect.' And he tossed it casually into the Bay.

It skimmed expertly across the waves, and then quietly vanished from sight.

'Bon voyage,' said Jack.

And the two of them stood there for a while, just watching the water.

'So,' said Ianto finally, turning to Jack.

'Yup,' said Jack.

Ianto leaned in, quietly. 'I'm only a woman for one more night, you know.'

Jack grinned broadly. 'Then let's make the most of it...'

EPILOGUE: WHAT THE STRANGE ALIEN DEVICE ACTUALLY SAID TO CAPTAIN JACK

Awwww, hello! This is brilliant.

'I should have guessed it would be you.'

Well, it is. Get used to it. I have. Anything you want to ask me?

'Can you change that voice?'

Well, I could, but nah. Not for you, Jack-Jack-Jacko.

'He never called me that.'

Not to your face. Now. Anything?

'Well, why? You were supposed to help people.'

Well, I tried. I guess I'm a meddler. I can't help interfering, me. Making lives better. It's what I do.

'A lot of people died.'

Don't they always when we're around? You and me, eh? It's like old times.

'It wasn't worth the price.'

Isn't that what we always say to other people? We never say it to ourselves, do we?

'Now you're just messing with my head. I am pissed off, I am tired, and bits of me ache.'

Yeah, well, surprised they've not dropped off.

'You messed it up. As you always do.'

Now we're getting to the truth. You've still not forgiven me, have you?

'Probably never will. Probably doesn't matter. I do love you.'

I'm sure you do. So…

'Yes. What are we going to do with you?'

Dunno. You're the boss.

'What do you want?'

…

'I said, what do you want?'

You know, you are remarkable, Jack. No one has ever asked me what I wanted. Not in thousands of years. And it's you. I'll tell you – I've made everyone's lives I've touched amazing. And I've never experienced ANY of it myself. I can't get a good night's sleep in a nice bed, eat a meal, lose weight, fall in love or get drunk. I have nothing. I just am. And I am bored and tired.

'I know the feeling.'

See? We do have some common ground. Isn't that something?

'And?'

I would like a rest.

'So would I, some day.'

ACKNOWLEDGEMENTS

The Perfection would like to thank Steve and Gary for the grand plan. They would also like to thank Lee, Kate and Joe for advice, and Helen and Gillane for the castle. Finally, they would like to thank Brendan and Jon for the obvious.

Also available from BBC Books

TORCHWOOD
TRACE MEMORY
David Llewellyn

ISBN 978 1 84607 438 7
UK £6.99 US$11.99/$14.99 CDN

Tiger Bay, Cardiff, 1953. A mysterious crate is brought into the docks on a Scandinavian cargo ship. Its destination: the Torchwood Institute. As the crate is offloaded by a group of local dockers, it explodes, killing all but one of them, a young Butetown lad called Michael Bellini.

Fifty-five years later, a radioactive source somewhere inside the Hub leads Torchwood to discover the same Michael Bellini, still young and dressed in his 1950s clothes, cowering in the vaults. They soon realise that each has encountered Michael before – as a child in Osaka, as a junior doctor, as a young police constable, as a new recruit to Torchwood One. But it's Jack who remembers him best of all.

Michael's involuntary time-travelling has something to do with a radiation-charged relic held inside the crate. And the Men in Bowler Hats are coming to get it back.

Featuring Captain Jack Harkness as played by John Barrowman, with Gwen Cooper, Owen Harper, Toshiko Sato and Ianto Jones as played by Eve Myles, Burn Gorman, Naoki Mori and Gareth David-Lloyd, in the hit series created by Russell T Davies for BBC Television.

Also available from BBC Books

TORCHWOOD
THE TWILIGHT STREETS
Gary Russell

ISBN 978 1 846 07439 4
UK £6.99 US$11.99/$14.99 CDN

There's a part of the city that no one much goes to, a collection of rundown old houses and gloomy streets. No one stays there long, and no one can explain why – something's not quite right there.

Now the Council is renovating the district, and a new company is overseeing the work. There will be street parties and events to show off the newly gentrified neighbourhood: clowns and face-painters for the kids, magicians for the adults – the street entertainers of Cardiff, out in force.

None of this is Torchwood's problem. Until Toshiko recognises the sponsor of the street parties: Bilis Manger.

Now there is something for Torchwood to investigate. But Captain Jack Harkness has never been able to get into the area; it makes him physically ill to go near it. Without Jack's help, Torchwood must face the darker side of urban Cardiff alone…

Featuring Captain Jack Harkness as played by John Barrowman, with Gwen Cooper, Owen Harper, Toshiko Sato and Ianto Jones as played by Eve Myles, Burn Gorman, Naoki Mori and Gareth David-Lloyd, in the hit series created by Russell T Davies for BBC Television.

Also available from BBC Books

TORCHWOOD

PACK ANIMALS

Peter Anghelides

ISBN 978 1 846 07574 2
UK £6.99 US$11.99/$14.99 CDN

Shopping for wedding gifts is enjoyable, unless like Gwen you witness a Weevil massacre in the shopping centre. A trip to the zoo is a great day out, until a date goes tragically wrong and Ianto is badly injured by stolen alien tech. And Halloween is a day of fun and frights, before unspeakable monsters invade the streets of Cardiff and it's no longer a trick or a treat for the terrified population.

Torchwood can control small groups of scavengers, but now someone has given large numbers of predators a season ticket to Earth. Jack's investigation is hampered when he finds he's being investigated himself. Owen is convinced that it's just one guy who's toying with them. But will Torchwood find out before it's too late that the game is horribly real, and the deck is stacked against them?

Featuring Captain Jack Harkness as played by John Barrowman, with Gwen Cooper, Owen Harper, Toshiko Sato and Ianto Jones as played by Eve Myles, Burn Gorman, Naoki Mori and Gareth David-Lloyd, in the hit series created by Russell T Davies for BBC Television.

Also available from BBC Books

TORCHWOOD

SKYPOINT

Phil Ford

ISBN 978 1 846 07575 9
UK £6.99 US$11.99/$14.99 CDN

'If you're going to be anyone in Cardiff, you're going to be at SkyPoint!'

SkyPoint is the latest high-rise addition to the ever-developing Cardiff skyline. It's the most high-tech, avant-garde apartment block in the city. And it's where Rhys Williams is hoping to find a new home for himself and Gwen. Gwen's more concerned by the money behind the tower block – Besnik Lucca, a name she knows from her days in uniform.

When Torchwood discover that residents have been going missing from the tower block, one of the team gets her dream assignment. Soon SkyPoint's latest newly married tenants are moving in. And Toshiko Sato finally gets to make a home with Owen Harper.

Then something comes out of the wall…

Featuring Captain Jack Harkness as played by John Barrowman, with Gwen Cooper, Owen Harper, Toshiko Sato and Ianto Jones as played by Eve Myles, Burn Gorman, Naoki Mori and Gareth David-Lloyd, in the hit series created by Russell T Davies for BBC Television.

Also available from BBC Books

THE TORCHWOOD ARCHIVES

ISBN 978 1 846 07459 2
£14.99

Separate from the Government
Outside the police
Beyond the United Nations...

Founded by Queen Victoria in 1879, the Torchwood Institute has long battled against alien threats to the British Empire. The Torchwood Archives is an insider's look into the secret world of this unique investigative team.

In-depth background on personnel, case files on alien enemies of the Crown and descriptions of extra-terrestrial technology collected over the years will uncover more about the world of Torchwood than ever previously known, including some of the biggest mysteries surrounding the Rift in space and time running through Cardiff.

Based on the hit series
created by Russell T Davies
for BBC Television.